GLIMMER TRAIN
STORIES

EDITORS
Susan Burmeister-Brown   Linda B. Swanson-Davies

CONSULTING EDITORS
Allyson Bourke   Roz Wais
Chanda Wakefield

COPY EDITOR
Scott Stuart Allie

TYPESETTING & LAYOUT
Paul Morris

ADMINISTRATIVE ASSISTANT
Kaylin Elaine Dodge

COVER ARTIST
Jane Zwinger

PUBLISHED QUARTERLY
in spring, summer, fall, and winter by **Glimmer Train Press, Inc.**
710 SW Madison Street, Suite 504, Portland, Oregon 97205-2900
Telephone: 503/221-0836   Facsimile: 503/221-0837
www.glimmertrain.com
PRINTED IN U.S.A.
Indexed in *The American Humanities Index.*

Glimmer Train (ISSN #1055-7520), registered in U.S. Patent and Trademark Office, is published quarterly, $32 per year in the U.S., by Glimmer Train Press, Inc., Suite 504, 710 SW Madison, Portland, OR 97205. Periodicals postage paid at Portland, OR, and additional mailing offices. POSTMASTER: Send address changes to Glimmer Train Press, Inc., Suite 504, 710 SW Madison, Portland, OR 97205.

ISSN # 1055-7520, **ISBN # 1-880966-46-8**, CPDA BIPAD # 79021
DISTRIBUTION: Bookstores can purchase *Glimmer Train Stories* through these distributors:
    Ingram Periodicals, 1226 Heil Quaker Blvd., LaVergne, TN 37086
    IPD, 674 Via de la Valle, #204, Solana Beach, CA 92075
    Peribo PTY Ltd., 58 Beaumont Rd., Mt. Kuring-Gai, NSW 2080, AUSTRALIA
    Ubiquity, 607 Degraw St., Brooklyn, NY 11217
SUBSCRIPTION SVCS: EBSCO, Divine, Blackwell's UK

Subscription rates: Order online (www.glimmertrain.com)
or by mail—one year, $32 within the U.S. (Visa/MC/check).
Airmail to Canada, $43; outside North America, $54.
Payable by Visa/MC or check for U.S. dollars drawn on a U.S. bank.

Attention established and emerging short-story writers: We pay $500 for first publication and onetime anthology rights. We welcome your work via our **online** submission procedure: **www.glimmertrainpress.com**

Glimmer Train Press also offers **Writers Ask**—nuts, bolts, and informed perspectives—a quarterly newsletter for the committed writer. One year, four issues, $20 within the U.S. ($26 beyond the U.S.), Visa, MC, or check to Glimmer Train Press, Inc., or order online at www.glimmertrain.com.

Dedication

Happy birthday to our wonderful, wonderful, wonderful father, who turns 86 on June 22, 2003.

We dedicate this issue—and so much more— to you, Pop (Susan)/Daddy (Linda).

Henry John Burmeister (born Helmut Johann Theodor Burmeister) at age 18

Linda & Susan

PAST CONTRIBUTING AUTHORS AND ARTISTS
Many of issues 1 through 46 are available for eleven dollars each.

David Abrams • Robert A. Abel • Linsey Abrams • Steve Adams • Diane King Akers • Susan Alenick • Rosemary Altea • Julia Alvarez • Brian Ames • A. Manette Ansay • Margaret Atwood • Kevin Bacon • Aida Baker • Russell Banks • Brad Barkley • Kyle Ann Bates • Richard Bausch • Robert Bausch • Charles Baxter • Ann Beattie • Barbara Bechtold • Cathie Beck • Jeff Becker • Janet Belding • Sallie Bingham • Kristen Birchett • Melanie Bishop • James Carlos Blake • Corinne Demas Bliss • Valerie Block • Joan Bohorfoush • Robin Bradford • Harold Brodkey • Danit Brown • Kurt McGinnis Brown • Paul Brownfield • Judy Budnitz • Susanna Bullock • Christopher Bundy • Jenny A. Burkholder • Evan Burton • Michael Byers • Christine Byl • Gerard Byrne • Jack Cady • Annie Callan • Kevin Canty • Peter Carey • Ron Carlson • H. G. Carroll • David Cates • Brian Champeau • Vikram Chandra • Mike Chasar • Robert Chibka • Carolyn Chute • George Makana Clark • Dennis Clemmens • Aaron Cohen • Robert Cohen • Evan S. Connell • Ellen Cooney • Rand Richards Cooper • Rita D. Costello • Wendy Counsil • Doug Crandell • William J. Cyr • Tristan Davies • C.V. Davis • Laurence de Looze • Toi Derricotte • Janet Desaulniers • Tiziana di Marina • Junot Díaz • Stephen Dixon • Matthew Doherty • Michael Dorris • Siobhan Dowd • Eugenie Doyle • Tiffany Drever • Andre Dubus • Andre Dubus III • Stuart Dybek • Wayne Dyer • Melodie S. Edwards • Ron Egatz • Barbara Eiswerth • Mary Relindes Ellis • Susan Engberg • Lin Enger • James English • Tony Eprile • Louise Erdrich • Zoë Evamy • Nomi Eve • Edward Falco • Anthony Farrington • Merrill Feitell • J.M. Ferguson, Jr. • Lisa Fetchko • Susan Fox • Michael Frank • Pete Fromm • Daniel Gabriel • Ernest Gaines • Tess Gallagher • Louis Gallo • Kent Gardien • Ellen Gilchrist • Mary Gordon • Peter Gordon • Elizabeth Graver • Jo-Ann Graziano • Andrew Sean Greer • Gail Greiner • John Griesemer • Paul Griner • L.B. Haas • Patricia Hampl • Christian Hansen • Elizabeth Logan Harris • Marina Harris • Erin Hart • Kent Haruf • Daniel Hayes • David Haynes • Daniel Hecht • Ursula Hegi • Amy Hempel • Andee Hochman • Alice Hoffman • Jack Holland • Noy Holland • Lucy Honig • Ann Hood • Linda Hornbuckle • David Huddle • Siri Hustvedt • Stewart David Ikeda • Lawson Fusao Inada • Elizabeth Inness-Brown • Debra Innocenti • Bruce Jacobson • Andrea Jeyaveeran • Charles Johnson • Leslie Johnson • Wayne Johnson • Allen Morris Jones • Thom Jones • Tom Miller Juvik • Cyril Jones-Kellet • Elizabeth Judd • Jiri Kajanë • Hester Kaplan • Wayne Karlin • Tom Kealey • Andrea King Kelly • Thomas E. Kennedy • Tim Keppel • Jamaica Kincaid • Lily King • Maina wa Kinyatti • Carolyn Kizer • Carrie Knowles • David Koon • Karen Kovacik • Jake Kreilkamp • Marilyn Krysl • Frances Kuffel • Anatoly Kurchatkin • Victoria Lancelotta • Jennifer Levasseur • Doug Lawson • Don Lee • Peter Lefcourt • Jon Leon • Doris Lessing • Debra Levy • Janice Levy • Christine Liotta • Rosina Lippi-Green • David Long • Nathan Long • Salvatore Diego Lopez • Melissa Lowver • William Luvaas • David H. Lynn • Richard Lyons • Bruce Machart • Jeff MacNelly • R. Kevin Maler • George Manner • Jana Martin • Lee Martin • Valerie Martin • Alice Mattison • Jane McCafferty • Judith McClain • Cammie McGovern • Eileen McGuire • Susan McInnis • Gregory McNamee • Jenny Drake McPhee • Amalia Melis • Frank Michel • Nancy Middleton • Alyce Miller • Katherine Min • Mary McGarry Morris • Ted Morrissey • Mary Morrissy • Bernard Mulligan • Abdelrahman Munif • Manuel Muñoz • Karen Munro • Kent Nelson • Thisbe Nissen • Sigrid Nunez • Ron Nyren • Joyce Carol Oates • Tim O'Brien • Vana O'Brien • Mary O'Dell • Chris Offutt • Laura Oliver • Felicia Olivera • Thomas O'Malley • Stewart O'Nan • Elizabeth Oness • Karen Outen • Mary Overton • Patricia Page • Ann Pancake • Peter Parsons • Roy Parvin • Karenmary Penn • Susan Perabo • Dawn Karima Pettigrew • Constance Pierce • Steven Polansky • John Prendergast • Jessica Printz • E. Annie Proulx • Eric Puchner • Kevin Rabalais • Jonathan Raban • George Rabasa • Margo Rabb • Mark Rader • Paul Rawlins • Nancy Reisman • Linda Reynolds • Kurt Rheinheimer • Carol Roh-Spaulding • Anne Rice • Michelle Richmond • Alberto Ríos • Roxana Robinson • Paulette Roeske • Stan Rogal • Frank Ronan • Elizabeth Rosen • Janice Rosenberg • Jane Rosenzweig • Karen Sagstetter • Kiran Kaur Saini • Mark Salzman • Carl Schaffer • Libby Schmais • Natalie Schoen • Jim Schumock • Lynn Sharon Schwartz • Barbara Scot • Amy Selwyn • Catherine Seto • Bob Shacochis • Evelyn Sharenov • Sally Shivnan • Daryl Siegel • Ami Silber • Al Sim • George Singleton • Floyd Skloot • Brian Slattery • Roland Sodowsky • Scott Southwick • R. Clifton Spargo • Gregory Spatz • Brent Spencer • L.M. Spencer • Lara Stapleton • Barbara Stevens • John Stinson • George Stolz • William Styron • Karen Swenson • Liz Szabla • Lois Taylor • Paul Theroux • Abigail Thomas • Randolph Thomas • Joyce Thompson • Patrick Tierney • Aaron Tillman • Andrew Toos • Pauls Toutonghi • Vu Tran • Patricia Traxler • Jessica Treadway • Doug Trevor • Rob Trucks • Kathryn Trueblood • Carol Turner • Christine Turner • Kathleen Tyau • Michael Upchurch • Lee Upton • Gerard Varni • Katherine Vaz • A. J. Verdelle • Daniel Villasenor • Sergio Gabriel Waisman • Daniel Wallace • Ren Wanding • Mary Yukari Waters • Jamie Weisman • Lance Weller • Ed Weyhing • Joan Wickersham • Lex Williford • Gary Wilson • Robin Winick • Terry Wolverton • Monica Wood • Christopher Woods • wormser • Celia Wren • Callie Wright • Calvin Wright • Brennen Wysong • June Unjoo Yang • Jane Zwinger

CONTENTS

N. S. Köenings

Ardennes, 1972.

N. S. Köenings was born in Belgium in 1970. She lives and works in Bloomington, Indiana. The story published here is, in slightly altered form, also the opening chapter of her novel-in-progress.

N. S. KÖENINGS

The Accident, or, The Embrace

*D*ar es Salaam, Tanzania 1974

By the time Gilbert Turner's wife had seen that the walnut-colored, scarlet-stippled log her daughter Agatha sat stroking on the banks of India Street was no log, but a leg which had come loose from its owner, it was too late for her to scream. Somewhere between her collar bone and chin a scream-shape came careening to a stop—and Sarie Turner gasped instead. The others had already done their screaming. A newsboy like an egret, head cocked, wading in the fallen ruins of the news. A woman the color of a cashew, grey hair parted sharply in the middle, hands frozen in mid-air. And a coffee salesman, rising like a puzzled *jinn* in smoke that wafted from his toppled coals. There was a plump and muted hush, and everyone was still.

Everyone except the boy to whom that log—no, leg—leg-log, log-leg—belonged. In fact, he wasn't really screaming. The sounds he made might not have been coming from his mouth at all. There slipped from other parts of him, as it does from some kinds of winged insects, a variety of thrums and squeaks. There was: a wincing from the shaggy head with opaque hair; a creaking from the thin-boy trunk and thigh;

Glimmer Train Stories, Issue 47, Summer 2003
©*2003 N. S. Köenings*

and a steady droning from the leg which he still wore. This he clutched, as if to keep it safe, with two surprisingly big hands. The sounds his body made, delicate and soft, would have put any scream to shame.

Sarie Turner hovered on the curb, a brown knuckle raised up to the hollow at the base of her tight throat, about to make a choice. Ten feet to her left, squatting heedlessly, so that her flowered panties showed, sat Agatha, three-legged now, and quiet. Agatha had not even thought to scream. Instead, she carefully rolled down the cuff of the blue sock at the end of that lost limb with both of her small hands. Apple-cheeks puffed out, rosy lips pressed tight in concentration, she was calm, overseeing a boy's leg in a purple square of city shade. To Sarie's right, the hot, sunlit side, was the one-legged, black-haired boy, whose squeak and drone she could tell were growing softer. Moreover, all around him seeped a hardy, sticky pool of red. It made Mrs. Turner think of sauces she wished she knew how to make. She felt a strong desire to ensure that that boy's hair and chest and thigh kept making hopeful tunes. It was a riveting, visceral desire, and this was odd, because Sarie Turner was not given to communion. But there it was.

Sarie Turner chose. She took a breath, and with an able, manly finger, tucked a strip of yellow hair behind one of her ears. She lifted one foot in the air, and prepared to take a step. She took a last look at her daughter. Agatha was fine. In fact, perfectly at ease, she had now set to unlacing the boyless leg's brown shoe, so that that foot could stretch its toes (Bata, direct from the factory, Mrs. Turner noted, thinking that if she ever had some money a pair of Bata espadrilles were on her shopping list). Sarie nodded to herself. She hovered briefly with one foot in mid-air, tall, pale, something like a hefty praying mantis, and reviewed the choice she'd made: Agatha would soothe the leg, and Mrs. Turner would take charge of that other, altered body. So be it. Un-screamed scream protesting, disappointed, in her belly, she set that raised foot down and lifted up the other. Then she took some rapid, crucial steps. In doing so, Sarie Turner would poke a hole in the fine membrane that keeps some people well apart from others and prevents the spilling of their stories into a great big, swirling mess.

She was not alone in moving at that moment towards the injured child. A neat huddle formed as she went towards him, hiding him from view. This made her feel that urge she had more keenly. A babble rose up from the hush. Some in the assembly whispered. They tried to ascertain whose fault it was. Busses were no longer what they had been, but, really, was that up-country driver drunk? Didn't this crazy boy have moms and dads and uncles? What had he been doing in the road? The coffee-salesman joined the group and ventured that the boy had been trying to hunt house-crows. The woman with the middle-parted hair offered up that boys these days really had no sense at all, coffee-man included. This said, she tried to focus her slightly crossed blue eyes back down on the boy, and set to smoothing down her sari.

Mrs. Turner hurried. With her orange flip-flops she deftly overstepped a heap of hard green mango peels, three-pointed lady-fingers that had fallen from the middle-parted lady's woven shopping basket, and a slingshot, which Agatha would later learn belonged to the little boy who whimpered in the road. When she arrived, those who had surrounded him parted like a sea.

The driver's tout, a thick boy with a twig protruding from his lips, a nightwatchman with a military cap, *rungu* nightstick slung over his back (a different kind of stump), a litter-woman now, palm-frond basket heavy on her head, the coffee salesman, the woman in the sari, and the newsboy whose papers were now swirling unattended in a sudden gust of wind—they all stepped back to make room for the madam. Some of them were skeptical, and wondered exactly what she thought she was about to do. And some of them imagined that she would have some knowledge to apply which they themselves did not.

People are often mistaken in this last, imputing foreigners with all kinds of expertise, and all in all giving them far more credit than is due. For example, Mrs. Turner did not have a bright Mercedes-Benz parked right around the corner, with which she could convey the patient to a fine, exclusive clinic. And she was not a doctor. Nor was she related to any presidents or football stars. She was not even English, as most assumed she was (what other nation, after all, would be brave and sure enough to send its folk out here?). But Sarie Turner, because she had once had some training, knew something about nursing. It was this, coupled with that other, inexplicable desire, that had made her set out towards him in the first place.

They watched her. She was big boned, topped with un-kempt, desert-colored hair. She was freckled everywhere, it seemed, and very tall, in a dingy yellow shift imprinted with blue roses. She landed near the little crowd and then hiked up that yellow dress to reveal light pink, pomelo-sized knees. Wild haired, legs exposed, she squatted in the center of the road beside the wincing boy. She had lost an orange flip-flop on the way. The litter woman (whose own flip-flops were blue) slid it over to her with an able, graceful push of her big toe. The basket on the litter woman's head did not register a tremble. The nightwatchman kindly brought the cardboard sheet he slept on when it was late and there was no one there to see. Sarie Turner sat upon it, stretched her own legs out, and crossed them in a strangely dainty way. She leaned over slowly, so that her own head cast a seeping shadow on the boy, and she began to whisper.

Who knows what she said. Certainly not, "Your little leg will cast a spell on my green daughter." Surely neither did she say, "Your father, fate be damned, will overturn my apple cart." In fact Sarie, who was still Belgian though she had left that place very long ago, had some difficulty with English, and could not have spoken quite so easily. But perhaps she gave him little secrets which he would grow up to use, as signposts. Small things, that make a child want to survive. "My Agatha likes very much the candy, wouldn't you like some?" Or, "Of course you want to stay alive so you can be big, resembling your dad." It's possible. In any case, she soothed him and made certain, in that way that people who have once been nurses understand, that he would not lose too much blood. She tore a length of cotton from her shift and made a kind of bandage.

Losing a leg is nothing to smile about, of course, but there was a kind of holy (or unholy) luck at work that day. Some able wrinkling of space and time, an orchestration. For example, in the neighborhoods between this corner, the light pink hunkered palace of the Theosophical Society, the clock tower with the four round faces that look every way at once, and the eggplant-radish-onion stands of old Kisutu market, there were at least three charitable clinics, generously financed by the Aga Khan. In fact, perhaps the Aga Khan himself, though surely only human, was sending waves of luck their way.

Aside from these conveniences of placement, there was a lucky object in the fray, perhaps the luckiest thing of all. On the third floor of egg-blue Mansour House, where a son had been through a great struggle to acquire it and to convince his aging mother that such things were signposts to the future, there was a brand new, shiny, black and boxy telephone. This mother looked up from her embroidery at the moment when the bus (emblazoned—just imagine!—with the very words that she was stitching out onto a yellow hanging she intended for her daughter: *Al-Fadhil*, The Kind One) came veering around the corner and knocked that foolish slingshot-aiming boy right off his little feet. *Al-Fadhil!* God's name on the bus and on the cloth! She saw this as a sign that the time had finally arrived to engage with that black box. It was time now to submit, succumb, and get ready to participate, knowingly, for once, in the larger, it-is-already-written, ultimately beneficent plan of God.

The stitching woman used the only number (also lucky) that she knew by heart, drilled as she had been by the efficient, modern son "in case anything should happen." And what a thing had happened! Her needlework set down, she reached out for the telephone. Click–click. The operator spoke. And she gave up the number of nearby, cool, Kisutu Clinic, where her dear son's new (and also modern, clever) wife had got herself a job. Click–click. Click. An unseen switchboard ticked and gave over to a clatter. Then an ominous, thick quiet. The stitching woman's gasp, and disappointment—but no, then, followed at long, impatient last by a creamy, rolling ring! The son's young wife (the clinic's fine receptionist: more luck) picked up at the first shiver of her own distinguished box, and listened as Bibi told her that a holy bus had smashed into a holy boy just outside their building. Exaggerating, but convinced, her husband's mother told her that the bus had sent that boy's four limbs aflying, each in one of the cardinal directions.

Thus Sarie Turner can only be credited with having made the boy more comfortable and perhaps (though it's hard to know for sure) with having stemmed his blood at an important juncture. Just as she was tying up the tourniquet and had laid a hand on the boy's damp and burning brow, a troupe of professional medical assistants, alerted by the stitching woman's call, arrived. Among them was a doctor who came swooping down upon them and very competently gave orders as his little group, without a blink or gasp, took the little boy away.

They also took the leg away from Agatha, who, although she did not complain, felt a protective pang and a little stab of anger. She did insist on tying the one shoelace up again, a skill that she had recently acquired while playing with her

12

father's single pair of "dressups." She laced it snugly, so the shoe would not be lost—although it was lost, later, at someone else's no less nimble hands.

Once the boy was gone, the nightwatchman was sent to fetch the father and tell him the bad news. The street, with all the things upon it, began to collect itself again. Those runaway screams, now reassured, slicked down their frightened hair and came peering out of cracks and holes. Some people shrieked in retrospect, and hooted.

Hussein's Food and Drink was open by this time, and the owner (not Hussein, but Iqbal), who had caught the end of the events—the boy lifted on a gurney, the coffee salesman insisting that the bus had appeared as though from smoke, a tall medical assistant with a gold pen glinting at his pocket stopping for a moment to greet the woman with the shopping bag and to inquire, with questionable intent, about her absent daughter—brought out a bucket full of passion juice and a set of shiny tumblers. For Agatha, who liked passion best of all, he even brought a straw. The litter woman drank without tilting her head back. The coffee salesman did not accept the offer, saying he preferred his own beverage to theirs. The newsboy got a refill. And the driver's tout, afraid that the next swooping of professionals might include the police, snapped his fingers twice and vanished. The driver had already slipped out of the bus, which blocked the street and would later cause a traffic jam and a series of commotions which are external to this story, and was making plans to head back to Morogoro, where he, too, would disappear.

About the shoe: the patient's father would complain to Sarie Turner—sensing even then that there was more to come between them and aware that his complaint might seem a little out of place, or petty, but unable to keep his indignation in—that while he had retrieved most of his son back from the doctor, he had not been given back the shoe. The doctor was embarrassed. For show, he bullied all the nurses right in front of the boy's father. The nurses quaked and trembled in the airy hallway, bit their lips in sorrow, and shook their well-trained heads. The doctor, despite his finger wagging, and one or two quick winks that he thought might at least produce a tale, could not extract from them an answer. He offered the boy's father his sincerest of apologies. "You must be looking now to what he *does* have left, I say," he said, laying an unwelcome hand on the anxious father's arm. "What's a shoe, *yakhe*, in the face of life, and death?"

In fact, what happened to that shoe is interesting: A young hospital worker, whose own father was a diabetic and had lost a leg—his left—to gangrene, took the shoe from the dead leg (which was a right leg, just like the one his father wore at home) in the night, imagining that it might fit his shoeless dad. It didn't fit, much to his shame. The worker had miscalculated. His father's foot was small, it's true, but not that small, and the shoe now sat smelly and accusing beneath the worker's bed at home, like a secret or a rotten fruit. But he was too ashamed to bring it back. Stealing a dead man's hat, or coat, might be one thing, but this! Stealing from the severed leg of a little boy whose other parts were very much alive! Well, that was harder to own up to.

But it was not a useless theft. In some ways, it was sympathetic sadness at the loss of that boy's footless shoe that helped bring Mrs. Turner to the very brink of love. She had a soft spot for Bata shoes, remember. "It is truly a surprise," she would say to Mr. Jeevanjee when she had heard the news, exposing one of her big knees as she reached for a *kaimati* ball the size of a small rose. "It is truly a surprise," Sarie Turner said, "the things which some of us are capable to do."

Sarie Turner, curious, already feeling cosmically entangled with the boy, and—more practically—badgered by her daughter, who had very fast developed a possessive love for that lost leg and wanted to see if it had been sewn back on to its owner, waited only a few days before going to the clinic to enquire if the boy was taking visitors. She had been initially dissuaded by her husband, Gilbert, who was scared and shy of unknown people, and masked his shyness with a show of expertise. He had said, among other things, "Muslims won't mix with the likes of us, my dear." He was reading a pamphlet that showed pictures of them, and had heard from the night watchman that that was what the Jeevanjees must be. And, "What will you do if they want—" he struggled, thinking. "If they want you *to take off your shoes?*"

Gilbert Turner considered himself the expert in the family. And families can only handle one. He liked to think that Sarie was a fragile thing, unsure of what she wanted, and that she needed him to tell her what to do. But she was made of tougher stuff than Gilbert knew, and could be single minded. Plus, to tell the truth, aside from giving music lessons every now and then, and making makeshift meals, she didn't have a lot to do. And Agatha had reached a restless age.

She said to Gilbert, "If they ask me to take off my shoes, I will take them off." Stepping ably from her rubber thongs, she set to demonstrating how this could be done. "It is not as if I had some sandals to unstrap. One, two." She did a little dance step on the blood-red rug. "It is not," and here she sighed, so that Gilbert wondered for a moment if his wife was bitter, and then decided she was not, "as if I had some stockings." She placed one of her big feet, now bare, onto Gilbert's lap. "See? It takes no time at all."

Gilbert looked up from his pamphlet and smiled indulgently at her. "Oh, Sarie." He wrapped a small pink hand around her ankle and looked up at her, thinking once again how tall this woman was. Somehow on their wedding day the flush of love had made her look much smaller. He knew she wanted shoes. "You just won't understand."

She leaned down from her great height and kissed him on the brow, where his thrilled hair was receding. "I understand much more than you can know," she said, and Gilbert misunderstood his wife as saying in this way that she forgave him for his joblessness, and that she didn't mind his wandering, or his staying home on afternoons, where he read books hand over fist, instead of making money. "I am taking Agatha today, and we will see that little boy." But Gilbert was back with the Dawoodis in his pamphlet, *His Holiness in Free Africa*, unaware that Mrs. Turner was on her way to finding out some holy freedom of her own. He himself was planning to go out in the early evening, reading done, to the Victorian Palm Hotel, where he might find a fellow ex-colonial who would be looking for a business partner. A person who might notice all the knowledge that Gilbert had to offer, and be prepared to take him on in some joint and reassuring venture.

Sarie put on her best dress, a light blue thing with small white dots, short sleeves, and a scooped neck. She dusted off a yellow vinyl purse. Into it she slipped a pen, and five pineapple sweets wrapped up in glossy paper. Agatha, seated on the bed and watching her tall mother in the mirror, mimicked her. She asked to be assisted with the zipper of her own best thing, a polyester shift with crimson radishes imprinted on its yellow folds. Sarie washed her hands. Sarie clipped Agatha's dark hair back with a plastic pin shaped like a lizard. Pamphlet on his chest and snoring lightly, Gilbert did not hear them leave.

On the streets the light was fierce and hard. Kisutu Clinic was pink and cool, and old. Sarie was happy to get out of the hot sun. Agatha blinked six times in quick succession, counting. In the new darkness of the clinic, after the brightness of the pavement, everything looked green. Sarie pointed Agatha to a set of wooden chairs lined up against the wall. Agatha sat quietly, peering up at two framed pictures of the Aga Khan, who looked healthy and avuncular, and was smiling sweetly down. Her feet dangled just above the speckled floor.

Smoothing her blue dress down over her belly, Sarie moved

up to enquire. The high fans on the ceiling wheezed. The receptionist, a narrow girl with fine, long hands, and a heavy pair of glasses over two round eyes, looked up at her and smiled, neat and patient. Sarie brought her pen out. Asked. Was answered. Listened. Nodded. At the advice of the efficient, narrow girl, Sarie wrote the following: "Tahir. Mahmoud. Jeevanjee. 10 yrs. Lives with Fthr. MG Jvnjee. Pemba House. Floor 2." The boy had been released.

The girl with glasses slid the papers she had taken out back into a file. Sarie noticed that her fingertips were stained bright orange. The cabinet closed with a soft click. The narrow girl looked across at Sarie, then away, thinking. She turned her head just slightly towards the open doorway, and Sarie saw a shard of street reflected in her spectacles. A transparent man moved, swift, across the lens, and pulled a cart behind him. A white Fiat, gleaming, swerved. The receptionist then turned to Sarie Turner. "You are sure you want to visit?" She enunciated each word very clearly, the way that Europeans often do when they are speaking to a foreigner. For her own part, she wasn't sure that visiting this boy would be such a good idea. "I am thinking, Madam, that this boy," she paused. "Well, this boy, maybe he needs a lot of rest."

Sarie was fastening her purse. She heard the caution in the slim receptionist's soft voice. She faltered. Gilbert's croons came crouching in her ear. She almost stepped away, considered saying, "No. No, I wanted simply just to ask." But she looked over at Agatha, who looked very peaceful there, intent on the framed pictures and the pink clinic's smooth walls. Sarie borrowed a little steadfastness from her own child. She turned again to the receptionist. She brought a finger to her ear and pried Gilbert's warnings out, then flicked them to the floor. "I am certain of it. I am sure." she said. Husbands. They have a way of making one uncertain.

The narrow girl considered Mrs. Turner. While she did so, the electric current faltered, and the fans failed with a thunk!

Sarie, Agatha, and the receptionist looked in unison at the ceiling, blinked. The girl sighed. Agatha scratched a bug-bite at her knee. The skin on Sarie's bare arms puckered. The high fans twitched, then started up again.

The receptionist was not concerned that this tall woman would not know where to store her shoes, nor that she might reach out for a biscuit with an unsuitable left hand. In fact, had the receptionist had to choose a side, a party in the possible encounter, she would, today, have had no trouble in uniting with this visitor, yellow hair and naked arms aside.

She had heard a thing or two about this Mr. Jeevanjee, and wondered, not without a pang of sympathy, how this woman would fare. People know each other here, remember, though it looks like a big city. And anyway, cities don't split people up so much as, at least out here, they mix them all together until some of them fall sick from having learnt too much about their neighbors, and dream of building for themselves a little house out in the country, where people will only come to visit if they have to. And Kisutu in those days, though it was all mixed up with all kinds of people in close quarters, was much more like a village—people all on top of one another, and the only difference was that your neighbors were above the ceiling or beneath the floor, instead of simply right next-door. In fact, in a city there are eavesdroppers of every kind on every side, as well as up and down.

So this daughter-in-law had heard the same things others did, and more, because her husband's mother (the woman with the telephone, you will remember) spent most days on her balcony or on her rooftop, from which she sometimes witnessed a great deal. And Bibi liked to talk.

Let's look at what the receptionist had heard from Bibi, what caused her to ask Sarie whether she was sure. First of all, MG Jeevanjee, a brother of the famous family's Zanzibari branch, and also related to the kingpins of the same, who for a long time ran Nairobi, was not, as his other brothers were, a prospering success. MG Jeevanjee was not a man for business. ("I know," Bibi had said, shaking with the special thrill of telling tales that go against the grain, "you're thinking, *But those Jeevanjees have got it made*. But sometimes luck is a much stronger thing than blood, just listen.") MG Jeevanjee had started out with an inheritance, a newspaper and a wholesale shop, bought with the proceeds of cloves. In his clumsy hands both businesses had failed. The wholesale storeroom was destroyed in one wet night by a storm with wings and fists which sent two dozen kapok mattresses sliding out into the streets to be borne off by the rain. The newspaper, which MG had thought to turn into a literary thing by paring down the sports and starlet pages, folded quickly after. No, this Jeevanjee was not a one for business.

In fact, MG was a bad-luck man, if such a thing there is. Someone, it was Bibi's habit to maintain, must have cast a bad eye on his mother, or slipped something in his food when he was young. "We thought," Bibi had gone on to say, "despite all that, that once he'd got himself a woman, things might settle down for him, go right." MG, as men do, fell in wondrous, heady love, and even managed to get married to the darling of his choice, who had, as luck (it seemed) would have it, fallen for him, too. And she cooked him up a batch of babies, all of them strong boys with heads for math and an uncanny money-making sense. By now, they made illicit money by betting with their friends on *kerem* games—and they had ways of making winners lose their stride and losers strangely shine like gold. "So the first sons had some promise, *mashallah*, though nevermind that on the Big Day they will be branded for their sins," said Bibi. "We thought, 'The sons survive,' 'She is beautiful and good,' 'MG has no more thriving businesses to lose.' We thought that things might be looking up for him." But bad-luck men don't turn good-luck just like that, and no one knows God's plan. When the love-of-his-life wife set out to get him a new baby, she died, just like that. And the bad luck people thought had gone away came right back then. "Since she died, I don't like to say it, God forgive me, but the man is bad luck, through and through."

On generous days the daughter-in-law thought that MG Jeevanjee's reported habits—his wandering the streets at night, his sleeping in all day, his occasional browbeating of passers-by, his periodic disappearances—were not bad luck coming back. They were, rather, signs of love and grief. She thought that if her man died one day like that (*How like his mama my boy really is,* she thought, *with those "you might think that"s, "but really"s*) without warning in advance, she might act strangely, too. That is what she thought when she felt romantic. Mostly, though, despite the popular opinion at the clinic that an eye's an eye, and there is just no accounting for some things, she did think there was something to be said for evil eyes and sticky spells. She thought bad-luck men should be kept at one's arm's length, at least: bad luck is contagious.

The receptionist was hearing her mother-in-law all over again, was musing, and had forgotten Sarie. Agatha had slipped down from her high-backed chair and, bored with the ceiling fans and quiet, had come to stand beside her mother. Agatha was small, and when the receptionist looked down she only saw pale fingers creeping towards her on the far edge of the counter, a tuft of dark hair just behind. The daughter-in-law shut Bibi's voice off in her head. The final thoughts she had about Tahir Mahmoud's father were the headlines of Bibi's own accounts: the first was "Dangerous." The last, imagined in high letters, bold, was "Unpredictable."

This is what she said to Sarie Turner, not meaning to say anything at all, but unable to stop herself, because in her mind she was sitting up on Bibi's balcony eating almond *barfi,* feeling the soft wind on her young face, and it was hard to tear herself away. The headline just slipped out of her. "He is unpredictable," she said. Mrs. Turner did not hear her right. She frowned, leaned forward. The receptionist sighed, and gave

Sarie the approval she desired. "Yes," she said. *Maybe*, she thought briefly, *this is Fate at work.* "Go then, it is kind."

Sarie's puckered flesh unpuckered. Agatha gave one last look at the smiling Aga Khan. She made sure that he winked back. She slipped a hand into her mother's palm. The narrow woman blinked, and added, encouragingly—because what else can you do when it has already been decided, than take a step or two to help destiny along?—"Pemba House. It isn't very far."

Sarie and her daughter stepped out of the cool clinic back into the glare. The receptionist craned her neck discreetly, and even rose up on her bare tiptoes to see if what they'd told her was still true. It was. Sarie Turner, though decked out in her best dress, was wearing rubber thongs.

Then she wound the crank up on the telephone and called her husband's mother. Bibi picked up on the third ring. "I'm getting used to this," she said, and the son's wife could hear that Bibi sounded pleased, imagined Bibi plump and happy on the yellow couch. The narrow girl put her elbow on the counter and settled in her seat. They talked it over. They wondered how this Mrs. Turner was going to be received.

Bibi promised to set her chair up on the roof and keep her eyes fixed on the back of Pemba House until the sun set. "That man," she said, thrilled, dismayed. "He's lost his mind already." The daughter-in-law heard Bibi shifting in her seat, digging into reminiscence. "When Suleimanji died, MG kicked Akberali out of Pemba House, because he wanted a donation! Told him he thought burials were a good-for-nothing waste of time! And those wild boys threw water down into the courtyard, so Akberali came home wetter than the sea!" Bibi purred. "He's capable, you know, of anything." And now a foreign woman out in *kandambili* shoes with the hot sun beating right down on her head—who knew how that had already fixed her brain? Who knew what MG Jeevanjee might do?

Bibi had finished that first embroidery (*Al-Fadhil*), and was now fastening the bright tail of a peacock onto an old sheet. She squinted at the bird and said right into the telephone, "Anything could happen."

Since that holy boy was hit by that big bus, predicted in her stitchery, her pins and thread box had taken on a strangely golden shine. When Bibi put the telephone away she took a hard look at that stitched bird and thought that its splayed feathers really looked quite nice. Well, she hoped this peacock would sit tight on the bed sheet, and not foreshadow anything. In any case, she didn't think that MG Jeevanjee had any preening left. Bibi didn't learn exactly what took place in Pemba House that day. But she was right about one thing: unpredictable it was.

Pemba House was one of those many pastel-colored, multi-story mansions that had sprung up all over Kisutu in the early middle of the century, when dreams were boiling and hopes high. They were built by eager and determined people whose grandmothers and grandfathers had struggled over pennies, but whose progeny had finally arrived. Their names bore witness to their history: Ashok Building, 1942. Hormuz Villa, 1938. Premji Mansion, 1951. Honesty House, 1954. Names of sons whose star charts showed that they could carry on the family trade, or, as in the case of Hormuz Villa, a bouncing baby boy who had at long last been produced after a great big pond of girls. Honesty House was a cry for help and a demand. Others, like Tanga House, and also Pemba House, were named after the places from whence riches came, from sisal, or from cloves. In the days before bad luck became (for some people) another name for Independence and the snatching up of lands and homes, they had been beautifully kept up. All of them were rich in windows, up to a dozen on a single floor, each with a fine pair of painted shutters. Some of them had turrets, or wide round bulges on the side, with windows just as curved. Others had high verandahs made of wooden slats, so that the ladies could see out and keep abreast of goings-on, without ever being seen.

In MG's father's time, the houses were the flowers of the city's heart, each one a light and lovely color set off by the sun. Hormuz Villa was once a buttery, soft yellow, Premji House a blue more tender than the sky, The Happy Building a mild rose-apple pink. And Pemba House, a particularly fine example of this modern architecture, had once been painted green—a powdery, pale color, like pistachio ice cream, or like a newborn's knitted socks. But on the day that Sarie Turner took her little girl to see the boy who'd lost his leg, Pemba House (1932) was well on its way down, and looked more like a ruin.

Thirty years of heavy rains had soured that first green, and now that it was no longer owned by any Jeevanjees, now that its tenants were a mixed-up bunch of people with only this one MG remaining, there was no money to be had for painting. The outer face was streaked with black, as though an enormous woman's eye had wept above it, and brought mascara coursing down the walls. The few remaining patches of that green competed now with soot and dust, and the dark residue of diesel fumes from all those city buses. Some of the shutters had fallen off and been picked up by passersby in need of kindling, so that from some windows dingy curtains billowed, or a homely darkness showed. The high verandah had lost many of its wooden slats. If a woman were to sit there, Bibi had once said, a bad-news boy passing on the sidewalk could look up there and see right into her skirt. From gouges in the house face, strange tufted grasses grew, and from the rooftop tendrils snuck from strong, unruly plants.

But the daughter-in-law was right. Pemba House was not far from the clinic. The lack of distance between these two important, fateful places played a role in making Sarie, from some angles, strikingly attractive. Sarie, who in the cool air of the clinic had felt her skin go cold, was, as they approached, only just beginning to feel the heat again. This lent a pearly sheen to her wide brow, and caused a shimmer at her upper lip. She was just a little damp, a little tousled. Agatha—because children who are accustomed to the weather don't feel the heat this way—was cool and dry, presentable enough. They stepped in front of that once perfect light-green house, and each one read the name and date out loud. "Pemba House, 1932."

Sarie coaxed the slip of paper from her purse. Confirmed. "That's it," she said. Agatha squinted at the paper, said, "It's on the second floor." So Sarie, a little nervous but determined, and Agatha, who from the first felt calm, that this was but one step on the stairwell of her destiny, took deep breaths and made for the far end of the house.

There was a metal door ajar, giving access to an alley and a courtyard. When Sarie and Agatha stepped inside they found themselves, although in the city, in a neatly private place. As though the street outside, with Hussein's Food and Drink, and with Kisutu Clinic—even with their own apartment, huddled at the top of an old house that might have once been not so different from this—were very far away. There was washing, and the dull smell of waxy yellow soap. Men's pale undershirts hanging like hung men. An orange gown with outrageous, ruffled sleeves. A violet skirt with pleats. There were flowers growing out of tins, scarlet "ten o'clock" roses that opened in the morning, violet brinjal blooms. A pepper plant.

A white cat came out from the courtyard corner with a wet look, an uneven, sooty coat, and several bald, slick spots. Agatha bent to touch it and it fled, a suspicious glow in its pale eye. From up above, in the still and ashy air that fills up city houses in the afternoon, a parrot hollered, "Who's there, who's there, who?" Agatha, with her sharp ears, imagined that she heard a scurrying of feet, and in her unformed story-eye she saw young girls with long dark blue-black braids move swiftly to a kitchen where they would deftly make some juice. She thought she heard a biscuit tin, with its soft, seductive scrape, being taken from a shelf. She was wrong, of course. Agatha, so early on, was not yet good at guessing what was there.

Mrs. Turner, stepping backwards, caught her flip-flop on a stone. Stumbling, she tilted her head back to look upwards at the second floor. "I am Mrs. Turner!" she called, answering the parrot. She waited, neck craned up. There did come a response of sorts. A lean boy, bright eyed and bare shouldered, hair shining with dressing, even in that dusty light, leaned out over the window sill and grinned. He spoke quickly, saying something that Sarie did not understand. Another stumble. Sarie swooped both hands down towards her hips and then back up again so that she would not fall. "We've come to—" But when she looked up again, the boy had disappeared.

There was a scuffling in the stairwell, a door slam. Two. The hot sound (Agatha imagined) of a boy pulling on a cotton shirt and buttoning it up as he moved down the steps. And then, beaming and smelling of freshly dashed-on aftershave (lemons, pepper, glue), Amin Jeevanjee stood before them in the vestibule that opened on the alleyway. Sarie thought that she should introduce herself again, but the boy showed them up the stairs instead, laughing, urgent. News travels, you'll remember. This must be the woman who had braved the road in her cheap shoes and whispered things into his brother's ear while that little girl of hers sat fooling on the sidewalk with his newly severed limb.

They did have biscuits, in the end. Another boy was sent out to the shops, and came back with a roll of Nanjis. The downstairs neighbor (named Maria, owner of that skirt and gown) was dispatched to make tea. And while preparations were being made, in an excited hurry, MG Jeevanjee was roused from a fat nap, and came out to greet his guests. A thin man, with haggard blue-black hair that had begun to grey, he came out from his bedroom in an undershirt and creased blue trousers, dazed. He rubbed his stubbled face with his right hand. He yawned. He cracked his bony jaw. Sarie Turner raised her eyebrows, drew her lips apart, and took a preparatory breath of the cool air, as though about to speak. Agatha stood still. She wondered where the parrot was.

When the boys had come, Jeevanjee had been dreaming a strange dream—a dream with a blue rainstorm, a brass coffee set with seven cups, a fountain pen, and a doctor in it, who had been stepping through the puddles. The dream was still so fresh with him that when he first spoke to Mrs. Turner he almost asked her if her teapot had suffered in the rain, briefly thinking that he might persuade her to buy a coffee urn with cups.

She leaned in towards him with her right arm outstretched, and MG felt, because in a dream anything can happen, that he had been approached by a giraffe, who quickly turned into a camel. How single-toned this woman was, so tall! In fact he had to tilt his head to look at her. When his eyes could focus clearly, he was startled by her freckles.

"We came…"

"Welcome…"

"Your son…"

"So grateful…"

"My daughter…"

It all happened very fast, and soon they were sitting down, and her long legs were too long for the space between the bright blue settee and the broken coffee table, so that she pulled herself backwards on the sofa and showed MG her upper thigh without intending. And he was sitting down across from her with a wall clock right above his head, its brassy pendulum swaying back and forth and glinting in the light, so that Sarie, dizzy from the steps, and from the surprise of having set out to do something and finding herself in the midst of it, thought that he looked something like an angel, what with that glow about his head.

Bibi would have liked to know—who wouldn't?—what they talked about. But she hadn't been able to see anything at all. None of them sauntered past the open window in the kitchen, from which sometimes Bibi thought she could make out if a person was a woman or a man. And nothing that happened took place outside in the courtyard. In fact, all that Bibi saw, or thought she saw, was the swirl of Mrs. Turner's dress as she positively skipped inside that house when they first came. "It was orange," she would say.

Well, first of all, the downstairs neighbor brought them tea in a red thermos, along with seven rare *kaimati* balls that she had been saving for herself. Sarie, who didn't get enough sweet things at home, ate four in quick succession while MG Jeevanjee talked about the shoe. She made her declaration, about "what some of us are capable to do," and Jeevanjee agreed. Then, suddenly hungry, too, he ate the other three.

The boys at first hung back in the hallway, watching, whispering behind raised hands. Ismail, the stoutest and most wicked, said a racy thing about Sarie Turner's legs and Amin gave out a giggle. MG frowned at them so darkly that they felt ashamed. Then, because their father was really, to all of their surprise, *talking* to this woman, they snuck up closer to the settee, listened, and finally sat down on the floor and watched them, sometimes making faces.

Certainly MG pulled out an old exemplar of the newspaper he had once owned. Sarie Turner was relieved. A newspaper, something perfectly familiar. He showed her, very serious, the poetry pages, and admitted, because there was something very sympathetic in his guest, that it was a secret pastime.

Sarie liked a man who made things. Her freckled face lit up. "You write verse," she said.

Jeevanjee demurred, raising one hand to his breast. An unexpected blush spilled out from his neck over his face, which
was shadowy, but like hers, also long. "No, I am not a poet—
no."

Amin, eldest, elbowed Ismail, stifling a laugh. But Sarie,
much later, would turn Mr. Jeevanjee into a troubadour in
her own imagination. She would remain privately convinced
until the day she died that the man she took on as her lover
spent much of his time composing *ghazals* in her honor, the
best of which he was too delicate to share.

The grown-ups talked. MG leaned forward to press the
biscuits on her, which she took because she thought it would
be impolite to turn him down. The *kaimati* balls had filled
her. She twitched a little on the settee, to find the right posi-
tion for her legs. She talked about her husband. When Mr.
Jeevanjee finally pulled the coffee table to the side so that
Sarie could stretch her feet out on the carpet and sit in greater
comfort, she looked at him with gratitude. Her eyes shone.
She thought, *This tired man is charming, although he could really
shave himself.* Sarie told him that she had been a nurse and her
husband once attached to the High Court. Then she asked
about his wife. MG told Sarie Turner that his wife was dead.
While he felt a little pang somewhere below his ribs and
cringed, when he unfurled himself again he was surprised to
find the pang had given way to a desire for a biscuit. Sarie
Turner pushed the china plate towards him so that he would
not have to reach across the table. He chewed, and swallowed.
Then he smiled and took another.

In the other room, Tahir Mahmoud Jeevanjee was sleeping,
his one-and-one-half legs covered by a heavy flowered sheet.
The older boys took Agatha, who had been sitting quiet all
this time, waiting just for this, to see him. They woke their
youngest brother up.

"Here," Ismail and Amin said together, hands clamped down
on the girl's shoulders, "is the last person to have seen your

missing leg alive." They had turned it all into a game. They
pretended to Tahir, who had been a trusting boy since birth,
that they would bring that leg back just as soon as it was
found. "Daddy still has friends in newspapers, remember.
They'll put ads out for you every day. Full page. Wanted: leg,
last seen on India Street." They elbowed one another, because there was only one newspaper in those days, and in it
MG had no allies. Agatha thought that their words might
make Tahir cry, but this is not what happened. As Sarie in the
sitting room was discovering a man who, bad luck notwith-
standing, would turn her life around, so Agatha found herself
embroiled in something just as grand. Tahir Mahmoud reached
out for her hand and pulled her close to him.

"It itches," he whispered, pointing to the sunken sheet beneath his knee. "Do you want to see?" And Agatha, who did
want to see, clambered up beside him, and his brothers elbowed one another as Tahir raised the heavy sheet and
showed their guest the bandaged absence that he sometimes
needed scratched. Agatha tugged a pillow from underneath
her host's small shoulders, and took it for herself. She raised
herself up on one elbow, and the boy made room for her.

Agatha asked him if it hurt. None of them had asked him
this before. Tahir was about to nod, to say that yes it did, and
very much. He almost wished to say that there were embar-
rassments attendant to having lost a leg, that the clever brothers
had to bear him to the toilet if he needed to expel a poop
(they did this with a sweet solemnity and a tenderness that
they had never shown him in his fully four-limbed days). He
almost told her that when the aunties came he knew they
came because they had to, because it was too, too terrible what
had happened to MG's little boy. And that he could tell from
how they spoke and passed each other bowls of cashews,
chomping, busy lips a-smacking, smacking, that they did not
hold out much hope. "Two cripples in the house, now, crazy
Jeevanjee whose mind should have a walking stick, and now!

Now *this!*" They whispered to each other. And sometimes they spoke their thoughts out loud when they thought he was asleep. Suddenly his brothers looked better to the aunties— even Aunt Shemsia, who prayed a lot, who was good, who people said was spoken to by angels—Aunt Shemsia had once said (was it just a month ago!?) that Tahir was the only hope, the only boy whose head for numbers might not send him down to Hell. And yet Shemsia just the other day had turned to Ismail and wise-cracking, thin Amin, and told these two that they were all their poor *baba* had left.

Agatha considered him, tugging at her bottom lip with a tooth that Tahir noticed was quite sharp. "Does it hurt?" she asked again. Tahir felt his thoughts well up, and his eyes grew tight and hot. He had been about to tell her. But he remembered what the aunties said (they had gotten it from Iqbal, at Hussein's Food and Drink). This was the girl who had un-laced and laced his shoe, done something to his body while the other parts of him lay well across the road. Aunt Yasmina, visiting from Kenya Coast where her husband ran a photo studio, had told Shemsia that this girl hadn't even flinched. That she had sat there on the sidewalk (with her panties show-ing!) and watched over his leg as though it were a sleeping child. This was not, Tahir thought quickly to himself, a guest into whose shoulder he could cry.

He swept his tears back with a blink and heavy lashes. "It doesn't hurt too much." He pressed his lips together so that his cheeks puffed out a little. Insisting, he said, instead, "It itches." He motioned to the space below his knee, beyond the bandage. Agatha peered down under the cool raised sheet and imagined that if his leg could be sewn back, the foot would reach just there, just to a far swirl of printed leaves. Tahir let the sheet go and it flapped softly down to rest on Agatha's bent head. She struggled briefly and pulled it back to show her face and look at him. "The bad thing," Tahir said—Agatha cocked her head at him. "The bad thing is that now I've lost my slingshot."

Sarie came to call her then, and Agatha slid off the bed, careful not to shift the mattress, so the boy would not feel pain. She looked at him and noticed how his eyebrows slanted down towards each other, pointing at his nose. She reached out and pinched his face, gently, just above his cheekbone. "You're lying." Her words sounded like a hiss. He squinted at her, sniffed. "It hurts," Agatha said. "I think it hurts a lot." Then she skipped away from him towards Sarie, and he reclaimed his pillow, frowning.

Sarie hesitated briefly before stepping towards the bed. They had come for his sake, after all. And yet now that she was in his room, Sarie Turner faltered. Out on India Street, she had touched him intimately, as we touch those who are unknown to us but whose pain is great enough to want immediate care: one dispenses with formality. But now she felt that he was owned, by his father, by the house, by the empty chairs that faced the bed, meant for visitors whose vigils were expected. She felt that touching Tahir Jeevanjee might require a permission from his father that she had not yet obtained. *He never knew his mother*, gloomy Sarie thought. *But there are other people who come in to watch him, and sit down.* She wondered if the guests were women, imagined an army of them, dressed in pinks, and blues—colors the Kisutu mansions had once been—petting the sick boy and laughing with each other.

The once-bright wife and the absent-present aunties formed a kind of knot in her. She knit her light eyebrows together. She wanted to behave in such a way that if MG Jeevanjee were watching—he wasn't; he was in the other room, eating the last biscuit, listening for the parrot's flutter—he would find her actions irreproachable and right. So she leaned over him and tugged kindly at the bedsheet, which he had pulled up against his chin after Agatha had slipped away. "I am sure that everything will soon be going well," Sarie Turner said. Tahir looked up at her and could not make out the features of her face. He noted only that her hands were freckled, and that she smelled like talcum—not the kind the aunties sometimes wore, which smelled of wood and roses, but like what mothers sprinkled on their babies, after they'd been oiled.

Aunt Shemsia had once said that British people expected you to thank them for the things they did, even if this meant showing them how much what they did meant, or even if what they had done was small, to be expected, and did not deserve a thank-you. He wasn't sure if this was true, and if it was, how Aunt Shemsia could have known. But he put his hands together on his chest, one palm over a set of small, still fleshy knuckles. He closed his eyes, and opened them, and thanked her. Sarie pursed her lips together and stepped away from him.

Agatha, also tugging on cool cloth, pulled at Sarie's dress and reminded her that there were five pineapple candies in her purse. Sarie gave them to her. Agatha took smart-mouthed Ismail's hand and opened it with hers, slipped the sweets onto his palm, then closed her fingers over his. The clever brother looked down in surprise, laughed, though she had made him nervous. "No telling what girls like that will do!" he later told his friends, who had never spoken to a white girl, though they saw some of them in smuggled magazines and in the photographs of movie stars from Hollywood that their uncles kept pinned up behind the counters in the *paan* shops. Agatha released his hand and pointed at the patient in the bed, who was feeling, like his father in the other room, a queer welling in his belly. He was watching Agatha intently. "They're for him," she told Ismail, with a warning look. "All five of them."

MG Jeevanjee walked down the stairs behind them, barefoot, but having slipped into a shirt with too-long, wrinkled sleeves. Sarie felt his eyes fixed on the middle of her back. At the bottom of the steps he stopped, and told them to come back to visit any time. That Agatha—he smiled at her, so that the corners of his eyes curved up—Agatha hadn't even seen the parrot.

Outside it was cool, and just beginning to turn a heavy evening blue. On the roof of Premji House, Bibi craned her neck and thought she saw a woman in a soft, light dress stumble in the alley.

When Sarie and Agatha got home, Gilbert, as predicted, had gone out. He wandered as he usually did along the waterfront, where the sea was low and flat, with the sharp green of floating seaweed and its jagged waves a hard metallic blue. Families from Upanga would be strolling now, heading for the cinema or to the Frosty for a sundae. The last of the onion-radish boys would be climbing into busses, and the last case of the day might be spilling from the courthouse. He was heading for the Victorian Palm Hotel where there might be gentlemen, maybe an old colonel or an Englishman just down from Kenya with some bright ideas. Someone, there— he smiled softly to himself as he smoothed his hair and checked the buckle of his belt—someone there might see him for what he really was, and offer him a drink.

Gilbert Turner went in the evenings to the Victorian Palm Hotel because the yacht club had been moved to the other side of Oyster Bay, and he could not afford a taxi. In the early days the club had been just there on the harbor, affording a perfect, lordly view of sparkling blue sea and of the hulking ships that moved wood, cement, and cashew nuts up and down the coast. The older clubhouse had once been painted dazzling white, with lyme, so white it hurt the eyes. In those days it was frequented by men who did things, who went into the interior and came out with tales about the natives and their ways, men who smelled of wind and faintly of tobacco, and of a strangely dainty, enviable sweat. Men who— Gilbert had thought more than once, with an awed tingling in his chest—men who smelled of History.

The new club was out of reach now, having receded from the city center just as the real colonials had receded, ousted from the courts and harbor offices. Those moneyed ones who chose to stay (who had had better jobs than Gilbert), now lolled, as the relocated yacht club did, in luxuriant repose in the northern suburbs, where the land was green. There were villas springing up out there, one by one, slowly but encroaching surely on the bush—gracious things, boxy, floored with speckled tiles and also rich in windows—surrounded by walled lots with lovely garden trees. When the remaining ex-colonials had picked up and settled out of town, Mr. Turner, more complex than one might think—a conflicted man despite his soft, weak look, and the tangy scent of failure that seemed to follow him around—took their tiny savings and moved his family to Kisutu, where they would be, he had said, "in the thick of things."

It was a moving in instead of moving out, and he had felt that in this way, in committing to Kisutu and its throbbing streets and shops, its mattress stores and bus stands, he might stake a small claim of his own on how things would develop. But one result of this move inward, which was all he could afford, was that when the yacht club snuck away from the main harbor, it also snuck away from him. And so he justified the Victorian Palm Hotel, where lesser men would gather.

There by the sea front those who lived close to town, those who didn't have a car, but who still had aspirations, gathered in the evenings for a drink. Tanzanians went, men with pens in their pockets and brassy watches on their wrists, and ties around their necks. Men with perfectly pressed pants. Gilbert found a sort of pride in this place, too. After all, he did have aspirations. Sometimes he would find another man like him who had not gone away when the end came, whose fortunes—though usually better than Gilbert Turner's—might at least not have soared. He might find Kazansthakis there, for one, although Kazansthakis's fortunes were really far better than they should have been, and far better than Mr. Turner's. Kazansthakis ran the Frosty Kreem near the sea, and had met his sweetheart there (another Greek, youngest child of prisoners of war who had, after another earlier end, also passed their expiration date). She had come in with her sister and ordered a tricolored (pistachio, vanilla, penicillin pink) scoop of cold, sweet stuff which she asked him, please, to cover up with syrup. Kazansthakis winked at her, and she winked back. Of course they fell in love.

Kazansthakis would pay for Gilbert's drinks and listen patiently while Gilbert told him what he'd read. Today, Gilbert thought, smiling to himself again, he might tell Kazansthakis about the Dawoodis in the pamphlet, whose Holiness had come from India on a tour.

In some ways, just like MG Jeevanjee, Gilbert was a dreamer. Kazanthstakis listened to him and never failed to say, "Mr. Turner, you were meant for greater things than this." That was when the Frosty King would start to shuffle in his pockets and signal to the waitstaff that it was time for him to go.

Gilbert did find Kazanthstakis there, that day. Kazansthakis would be there all week, while the Frosty was remodeled. So meeting at the Victorian Palm Hotel became for them a small routine. For five afternoons that followed one another, each one of which brought Mrs. Turner closer to the brink of things (life, love, danger, hope), Sarie Turner's husband sat at the Victorian Palm and told Kazansthakis stories which he had taken from his books. And that week in Pemba House, where Sarie and Agatha stayed later and later every time, another, more complicated schedule was also ratified.

Day one: "The places where Sikhs died along the railway line have now become famed shrines." Kazansthakis was amazed. *Agatha met the parrot, and stood beneath its gently swaying cage in awe.*

Day two: Gilbert said, "The White Father Missionaries wore white dresses in the hopes of being taken for a troupe of

Mohammedans. This peculiar outfit has now become their costume." Kazansthakis liked this one so much that he bought another round. *Sarie Turner convinced MG Jeevanjee to read to her from his favorite issues of the long-dead paper. He read a poem called "The Pomegranate," and then, to cool the air and set things back on a more ordinary course, he read another, "Cat, the Thief of Meals."*

Day three: Gilbert said, "When Nkama Ndume, local king in Pemba, Zanzibar, lost his temper with his staff, he made women sweep the kitchens with the pillows of their breasts." The Frosty King gave this one a laugh. Then, inexplicably, he blushed. *MG Jeevanjee revealed that as a child in Zanzibar he had played football by the sea. Sarie confessed that, although she was Belgian, she did not know how the game was played.*

Day four: "When Livingstone died they left his heart in Zambia, put his lungs in Zanzibar, but they took his corpse to England." Kazansthakis, like everyone else, had heard this one one too many times, and did not believe it anymore. "Tell me another one," he said. *Sarie Turner found herself nodding on the tiny sofa, wondering why she was so tired. MG Jeevanjee, forgetting who she was, suggested that she just lie down and take a nap. This is what his dead wife might have suggested. This time Sarie blushed, and did her best to stay awake while Agatha watched Tahir in the other room.*

Day five: Mr. Turner, on his second drink, confessed to Kazansthakis that, despite what everyone might think, Gilbert Turner was much more of a thinker than a doer. That he would like to think and dream his life away. Kazansthakis coughed and motioned to the sea, where fishermen were just preparing to go out again in narrow boats. "And what a life we have, old man," the Frosty King suggested. *Agatha watched Tahir sleep, fifth day. His wounds were healing. He lied less and less when he told her that it did not hurt. Sarie and MG Jeevanjee found themselves alone in Pemba House's hallway.*

They had just come from the balcony (that high verandah

through the boards of which Bibi said some underwear might just be seen), where Jeevanjee had pointed out the seedlings he was hoping to transplant one day to the courtyard—a coconut palm, a pomegranate tree, and a little henna bush, in a variety of broken pots. Sarie said something about wishing that she had a garden, and Jeevanjee, eyes moist, feeling that he already had his toes over the edge of a great precipice, said, "Mrs. Turner, I am making a garden of my own, right here in the city center! And any time, oh, any time at all—"

He wrung his hands, chest full of rich emotion. Sarie turned those light blue eyes on him and raised her eyebrows. She lost her footing momentarily and had to steady herself on his arm. His elbow was sharp, but just above it beneath the cuff of his pale shirt there was a plumpness that she found surprising. Jeevanjee looked up at her and barrelled on, brave, sincere. "You can come here to my home and we will bring a chair for you to sit on the verandah."

She nodded at him, awed by kindness. She followed him inside where something about the velvet air was blue. The door to Tahir's room was closed. Ismail and Amin were out. Sarie had been looking at the back of MG's head, sucking at the inner flesh of both her cheeks at once, biting softly down. Considering. *How blue the light is,* Sarie thought. *How nicely Mr. Jeevanjee is swaying now as he moves forward in the hall. One would say that he is like a reed at the edge of a green pond.* And she felt a fierce, sharp tingle come tripping up and down her limbs.

When Jeevanjee turned around to look at her, meaning to say, "And now may we have some tea, I will call for...," he caught her looking at where the back of his own head had been, now right into his eyes, and she turned the rich plum color of Ribena Concentrated Syrup. Jeevanjee felt a stab of fear inside of him, and, with a little yelp, he pressed himself suddenly and unexpectedly against her, because he was too cowardly to mark the slow and tender steps it might have taken otherwise. Later he would be able to think to himself, " I don't know how it happened." And, when he felt remorseful, "*I* didn't have a hand in *this*." Of course he had a hand in it—two even, which wrapped themselves around Sarie Turner's sinewy, long throat, and then, riffling as though through a drawer to find the urgent thing, across her back and then around her trunk to part the curtains of her dress and feel her freckled flesh come loose and tepid in his palms. It was easier to do it all at once.

Curled up inexplicably on the great wooden bed she shared with Gilbert, Sarie later wished that it had all been slower, so that she could make a list, a calendar of small events—*first he, and then I, and then he, oh yes. And then I, yes, and then we and then I and then he again and I knew and he touched and I and we and then he, and by then it was too late.* Sarie would have liked to savor it, while Jeevanjee wanted to forget how it began, and feel himself already in the midst of it, already at sea, and too far from the shore. The shore: the aunties, Shemsia with her enormous eyes and spotless reputation, the thievery of his two-legged sons, the photograph he had of himself standing beside his beautiful first wife at a picnic they had gone to on the beach at Oyster Bay, the ruins of the newspaper, old issues of which he forced himself to read, Akberali, and how frightened he had looked with water on his head, and the fact of his now mangled little boy, and everything, everything else that he was trying to forget.

In any case, at sea they were. Sarie mimed the movie actresses she had seen once or twice in films at the cinema beside the Frosty Kreem. She moved her lips softly in the air. She kept her eyes closed, expecting that eventually she might feel Jeevanjee's warm tongue against her lips, and, bending down to match him, press her brow against his neck, and sigh. Jeevanjee focused on Sarie Turner's chest and belly, which he rubbed, she thought, like the lamps she read to Agatha about, from which spirits come. To Jeevanjee, the space between her shoulders and her hips seemed vast.

While the embrace, sudden, hectic, endless, wound up and on and around the parents in the hallway, Agatha watched Tahir. And because sometimes mothers and daughters are linked in secret ways, Agatha felt a hot coal in her chest, a thick confusion, which echoed Sarie's shock and shivering in the hall. She thought for an awful moment that she felt this way because perhaps Tahir had died.

As MG Jeevanjee, failed businessman and poet, pulled Sarie Turner across the vestibule so that he could lean her up against the peeling wall and reach her corners better, Agatha was pulled out from her chair to the edge of the soft bed, where, chest tight and burning still, but thrilled, she heard little Tahir snore. While Sarie bent her knees on the other side of that room's door, so that Jeevanjee would not be daunted by her stature, Agatha listened to Tahir Mahmoud's breathing. Eventually she was so lulled by it that she closed her eyes and went to sleep.

When Sarie came to wake her, Agatha felt fresh and glad to see her mother, as though she had woken from a lovely dream. Sarie was no longer flushed. Her yellow hair was dark now, that peculiar shade of green that some blondes generate when their hair has gotten wet. She had just thrown water on her face, brought to her by Jeevanjee in a shiny metal bowl. Jeevanjee had watched her pour the water with a cup over her high cheeks, and had wished that she were standing naked there instead of in that horrible old dress, and that he could watch the water trickle over her long body—of which he was already irrevocably dreaming, and enamored, though he could not fathom how it would really look.

Sarie leaned over Agatha, and though she was no longer flushed, her freckles twinkled. "We have already stayed enough," she said to Agatha, hurrying her up. "When we get home," she paused, stroked her daughter's brown shoe-polish hair. "When we get home, your father will no longer be there."

She meant that Gilbert would have already headed for the watering hole. But she was correct, of course, also in another way.

Gilbert, the Gilbert that she knew, from that day on began to shift. He was on his way to hovering, to wobbling in the wings of rooms. He was on the way to growing softer, sweeter, once his edges blurred. And he only came into sharp focus for Sarie Turner if Jeevanjee was there, hair combed, and smiling at her husband as though he were his greatest, truest friend.

In a way he was. Gilbert and Jeevanjee found that something in their natures bloomed in the fresh light of the other's unexpected company. Perhaps Sarie was not, as she thought to herself at first, careening cosmically into the arms of a man who was entirely different from her husband. The two men, it turned out, had quite a bit in common: for one, a love of cars, something both of them had long kept only to themselves, and which, once confessed, was met by everyone with great surprise. When that business opportunity Gilbert had been itching for arose, this unsuspected inclination would stand them in good stead.

Jeevanjee was an answer to their prayers: Sarie, who dreamed of brash and unforgiving love, and of shopping lists that did not end in tearstained crumples on the floor; Gilbert, who dreamed of a pleasant, easy business venture which would permit him to get his wife some shoes; and Agatha, who, while never a gregarious child, had often dreamed of parrots, and was pleased to have a friend in Tahir.

Tahir and his brothers were amused by Agatha. The older boys made jokes about her mother, at which, Tahir would maintain ferociously when he went on to court a bony, lightly freckled woman of his own, he himself had never laughed. Jeevanjee, though he knew that he was tempting fate, felt he had at least, at last, found someone who could bear to hear his poems. Bibi would find enough in all of this to feed twenty-seven years of pleasure. Despite the dusty town, and the way the buildings crumbled, and the way the shops dried up for the endless lack of goods, all of them, in this corner of Kisutu, would feel fairly rich in love, and be enfolded, temporarily at least, in the promise of a new prosperity.

Chieh Chieng

A nice day at the park. I was probably complaining about something.

Chieh Chieng is currently completing his MFA in fiction at the University of California, Irvine.

CHIEH CHIENG
The Exile of Calvin Wu

FIRST-PLACE WINNER
Short-Story Award
for New Writers

*J*he year China reclaimed Hong Kong, Calvin turned fifty-eight, and was sent into early retirement by his boss. Soon after, he asked Dolly to consider quitting the Waterfront Hilton, where she was executive chef, and join him at home. He fantasized about fishing marathons at the Huntington Beach pier, baking parties, and falling into sleep with his wife, drunk from one of her triple-layered Swiss chocolate cakes.

"I'm happy enough seeing you in small blocks of time," she said.

She continued waking each morning at five sharp for work. He'd warm up her car's engine while she ate breakfast and repeatedly told him to go back to sleep. When she came home, he'd have a hot cup of tea and the day's paper waiting for her. He'd start the rice while she read, and she'd cook the accompanying dishes when she was ready, simple sprouts and assorted leafy dishes with quick prep times and low cholesterol content.

Glimmer Train Stories, Issue 47, Summer 2003
©*2003 Chieh Chieng*

Calvin kept busy to avoid loafing around the house and thinking, because each time he got to thinking he thought about Dolly and his son Arnold, who had jobs to stay busy with, and his parents, both buried in Malaysia. Everyone else seemed better occupied.

Mornings he fished for mackerels at the pier, and painted. He started with barns and lush forest paths because that was what the old woman on PBS painted.

After two snowy cottages, Calvin poured on the yellow ochre and burnt sienna, covering the canvas in a sun-drenched landscape. Hours later, he had a portrait of a Malaysian stilt house with several fighting cocks in the foreground.

The house, which he'd last seen in person nine years ago, was Uncle Toh's. Only a few years apart, the two men wrote each other often, with his uncle usually raving about whichever new woman he was seeing.

When Dolly returned from work, Calvin asked, "What do you think?"

She nodded.

"Okay?"

She nodded.

"Should I throw it away?"

She shrugged.

"A stilt house," he said.

"Haven't you seen enough of them?"

"I'll paint a picture of you if you're not happy."

"Don't paint one of me now. Paint one of me in my high-school uniform."

"You don't look bad now."

"Start the rice."

At fifteen, Dolly moved from Hong Kong to Sibu, where she stayed with an aunt who usually never knew where she was or even when she was gone.

She'd already made plans. She wanted to move to California and work hard so they could buy a vineyard. She'd read the first hundred-fifty pages of *The Grapes of Wrath* for English class and felt inspired. She told Calvin that after college they would marry and follow the way of the Joads to financial success.

When he announced the engagement to his parents, Ma said, "Your home's here. Did she suggest moving?"

"Mutual decision," he said.

"She suggest it?" Ba asked.

Calvin nodded.

They said he had no reason to go leaving the country when his parents were here. Who would watch over them when they got old? What if they fell, or accidentally stabbed themselves with some yard tool, and there he was, thousands of miles away? Didn't he realize they'd been looking for an affordable house and wife in the nearby towns for him?

"Girls from Hong Kong would sell your arms if they could." Ma tapped her head. "You were never too strong up here. We would have been happy with a dumb girl. Then you could make the decisions."

They told him to break it off with Dolly. They'd thought she was only a temporary thing. When he refused, Ma sat him down and said she once had an older brother who married a girl from Hong Kong. After the marriage, the couple moved to Kowloon, where the new bride ran off with an old boyfriend. Heartbroken, Calvin's uncle returned to Malaysia and threw himself into a river. It was the southwest monsoon season, and the rain didn't let up. The river raged for weeks and erased every trace of him. "My parents," Ma said, "never smiled again."

"What was my uncle's name?"

She hesitated. "His name was Your Uncle."

"There's no uncle."

"Because he's dead!"

He got up to leave.

"Don't go," she said. "Why do you want to go?"

He shrugged because he was ashamed to admit he was just following Dolly, that if she wanted to harvest litchi in Singapore, he'd be game.

Before he left Malaysia with his new bride, his parents said, "She'll never be welcome in our house."

Calvin thought they'd change their minds. Each year he wrote asking if he and Dolly could visit, and each year they said only he could. After Arnold was born, he wrote saying they wanted to visit as a family. His parents wrote back, "Your son will always be welcome, and even though you've done nothing but disappoint us, you can come, too."

He didn't want to visit without Dolly even though she'd told him to just go without her. He wanted everyone to be together in one room, his wife included. If Ma and Ba wanted to be stubborn, then he wasn't going to budge either. Their capitulation he always thought certain, and coming within the year.

Ba died first and Ma hardly spoke to Calvin when he returned for the funeral. When she did speak, she'd say, "Too bad you didn't come back when he was actually alive," and he kept his mouth shut, because she was right.

Ma pretended not to notice Dolly, and spent most of her time talking to Arnold in Fukienese, even though Calvin had explained that his son wouldn't understand a word. "Cousin Shan," Ma told Arnold, "married a woman from a headhunter tribe in Borneo and came back missing a leg." Arnold nodded sternly. He was thirteen. Calvin doubted the existence of Cousin Shan, but kept quiet because Arnold didn't understand anything Ma said anyway.

Ma died a year later and Calvin returned to burn incense and bow three times in front of his parents' stones. Dolly, whose parents were Buddhist, suggested bringing fruit as a sort of housewarming gift for the dead. Calvin didn't see the point, but agreed to it, so Dolly placed mangoes on a paper plate in front of the headstones, and they watched the fruit bake under the sun.

Most of the afternoon he shooed large mosquitoes away from his wife and son. One of them bit Arnold's right hand and turned it into something bloated, red, and round.

"Your parents' anger." Dolly held the infected hand in hers, a desperate look in her eyes. "And I even brought food." She thrust Arnold's hand in Calvin's face. "Tell them not to take it out on my son."

Calvin didn't know what to do except curse the mosquitoes. His parents couldn't make a mosquito bite his son any more than he could make the swelling go down right at that moment. The dead don't command insects, and the dead don't eat.

All he could do was stand next to a pair of stone tablets and watch Dolly drag his boy away in search of a clinic. All he could do was follow.

He wanted to see Ba again. He wanted to listen to another of Ma's cautionary tales starring imaginary relatives, because their failures granted him relative success as a son. So he missed being at his parents' deathbeds, he kept telling himself. At least he had both his legs.

He began painting his parents. He painted them glaring while watering plants, glaring while shopping in the local market, and glaring while rowing a boat on the Rejang River. He painted them like this because he couldn't imagine them looking any other way.

"Are they squinting?" Arnold asked.

"They're angry."

"Because they can't see?"

"Angry at me," Calvin said.

Arnold shrugged and grabbed a popsicle from the freezer. He sometimes came over after work or on weekends to eat what was in the refrigerator, which Dolly kept packed with his favorite junk food.

And their suppers. On the nights Arnold ate with them, their suppers became feasts again, feasts in which Calvin re-acquainted himself with old friends such as Dolly's profoundly moving halibut stew and her refined, yet sensible porterhouse. Otherwise, she cooked simple steamed vegetables or tofu, and it was the promise of better food that usually prompted Calvin to invite his son over.

They were eating seared rabbit loin over arugula and truffle dressing when Dolly said, "All these damn paintings."

"Don't say 'damn' about my paintings. They're of my parents."

"They said more than 'damn' to me."

"I'm saying don't curse my parents."

"The goddamned paintings."

"They took care of me for twenty years."

"And I did nothing for thirty-six years?"

"I left them for you," he said.

In the brief silence that followed, Arnold stood quietly, thanked Dolly for the meal, and sped away.

"Malaysia is nice this time of year," she said.

"It's the monsoon season," Calvin said.

"It's always the monsoon season."

"Can't I paint some pictures of my parents?"

"They never would have brought fruit to my grave."

That he couldn't argue.

"I'm not your guilt urinal," she said. "You feel bad for leaving them, then go. Visit their graves. Clear your conscience there."

"I don't want to go," he said.

"You're going."

"What if I say no?"

"I'll leave you."

It took Dolly a day to find him a competitively priced ticket to Malaysia. There he would stay with Uncle Toh, and she would send money every two weeks to cover living expenses. It wouldn't cost much for him to live comfortably, she said, considering how weak the *ringgit* was against the dollar.

"Wife sending you away?" Uncle Toh asked on the phone.

"Just visiting," Calvin said, his parents' Fukienese dialect easy on his tongue despite years of dormancy. He'd spoken Cantonese with Dolly and English with Arnold all these years, but the Fukienese was something he'd never forget, even though it only reminded him of regret, like an ex-girlfriend's face or a case of food poisoning.

"I'll line up the most handsome divorcees and spinsters for you," Uncle Toh said.

Calvin thanked him and hung up. "How long am I staying?" he asked Dolly.

"Until you've cleared your conscience."

"That takes how long?"

"I haven't decided yet."

Calvin called Arnold immediately. "It's a one-way ticket, son. It's really one way. Come here after work."

That night, Arnold asked Dolly what Calvin told him to ask.

"He can't stay with you," Dolly said. "His parents are in Malaysia."

"You won't have to see him." Arnold sat next to his father.

"He needs to resolve difficult turmoil in his heart," Dolly said.

"Difficult turmoil?" Calvin asked.

"He is haunted by ghosts," she said to Arnold. "He has to say goodbye to them before he can come back. There is no room here for ghosts."

The night before his departure, Calvin asked Arnold to speak to Dolly again.

"I already tried," Arnold said. "Why would she listen to me?"

Who does she fill the refrigerator for? Calvin wanted to

ask. Who does she grill salmon steaks for? "Just do it," he said. "Tell her how sad you'd be if I left."

There was a long pause.

"Fine," Arnold said. "Maybe she'll listen."

"Don't buy me any gold," Dolly said on the way to the airport. She kept gold bracelets and earrings in a safety deposit box at the bank, and Calvin had been planning to add to her collection on his eventual return.

She'd ask him to come home soon enough. She had to. He was her husband.

She sat up front with Arnold. Calvin sat in the back and watched familiar buildings and stores pass, the Albertson's he shopped at, the *pho* restaurants and art supply shop he already started to miss.

"It's so cheap there," Calvin said.

"No. And don't send any gifts. No postcards. No souvenirs."

"Gold's cheap there," Arnold said.

"Drive," she said.

At the terminal, Calvin hugged Arnold and thanked him for taking all the paintings back to his apartment.

Dolly shook Calvin's hand and backed away when he moved in for a kiss.

"No kisses," she said, but she didn't resist when he brushed her forehead.

"Time to go." She bit her lip, turned, and started walking. Arnold looked at him, eyebrows twitching, urging him to say something.

Calvin shouted, "Your hair!" Dolly stopped.

He panicked. The pressure to nail the perfect parting compliment was overwhelming. "It sparkles like a red snapper's scales!"

She moved forward and kept moving. Arnold mouthed to his father, Good job, and shook his head.

Seventeen hours later, Calvin still felt stupid for the comparison he made, and he could still see clearly the suggestion of a smile in the line of her mouth, something bittersweet.

Heat rippled off the tarmac and soaked into Calvin's body as he stepped off the plane. He was tired. He'd flown into Kuala Lumpur on a 747, but transferred to a small propeller plane for the bumpy trip into Sibu.

He slung the duffel bag over his shoulder and dragged the mini-traveler, its wheels squeaking along the concrete. He remembered his last visit and the effort Dolly made at warding off the tropical sun with her umbrella, and how happy she was to return to the mild warmth of southern California.

Uncle Toh stood just outside the terminal, waving. Next to him was a woman, and as Calvin approached, he noticed that she appeared to be in her late forties. Homely looking. She might or might not have been wearing makeup. He didn't care.

"Put your bags down," Uncle Toh said. "This is Ah-Ping. We've been together eleven months."

"Congratulations. Long time."

Uncle Toh smiled proudly. "You eat?"

Calvin shook his head. He wanted to run across the tarmac and jump back into the plane.

Uncle Toh put an arm around him. "Don't look so sad. You'll get used to being here again."

The one big road that ran from the Sibu airport snaked through towns with two-story shops that sold the electric scooters and bicycles most people still used for transportation. Calvin also saw a McDonald's, a KFC, and more cars than he'd expected.

First thing he did when he arrived at his uncle's house was ask to use the phone. He called collect.

"I landed safely," he said.

"Good," Dolly said. "No more phone calls from now on unless you need more money or get sick."

"Wait."

"You have things to do," she said. "And collect calls cost a fortune."

"Say something. If I get bit by a viper tomorrow, this will be the last thing you say to me."

"Take care," she said and hung up.

"Would you like shrimp for lunch?" Ah-Ping asked.

"Anything's fine."

Lunch wasn't anything to write about.

What Calvin wrote was an apology. "I should have compared your hair to something else," he wrote. "Something not food." He wrote that he missed her and looked forward to the day he could come home.

He sat proofing the letter until Uncle Toh came into his room and announced, "Tomorrow we'll have beef satay and your heart will feel better."

Beef satay was good, but did not make his heart feel better. Uncle Toh had bragged about the thick, subtly sweet peanut sauce at the local food stand, and sure, Calvin could discern a fine blend of brown sugar and cumin. But the sauce lacked panache, and peanut sauce without panache was like sweet-and-sour pork with no zip.

Uncle Toh tore a strip of beef from his skewer and chewed heartily. "You can't get this anywhere else. Enjoy it while you're here."

Calvin bit a piece off his skewer.

"You should make plans," Uncle Toh said. "Do something. Go places."

"I want to visit my parents."

"That's something, I guess." Uncle Toh swallowed and grunted. "You forgot what good satay tastes like."

Calvin bristled. "I know what good satay tastes like." He took another bite and shrugged to indicate mediocrity.

The cemetery was three square miles enclosed by a steel fence. It had been packed with the dead for many generations, and only because it included several hills could it accommodate as many as it did.

Calvin was exhausted and sticky by the time he reached his parents' stones near the top. He'd slapped his arms red keeping the mosquitoes away. They buzzed all around.

He'd been sweating nonstop since he landed here. Even the nights were warm and moist and he didn't know how he could have grown up in this heat.

This time Calvin brought neither incense nor fruit. He brought his red-streaked arms, his shirt smelling of his meaty body.

Dirt and rock had caked up the engraved characters of his parents' names, so he took off his shirt and wiped with it. He blew away small clods and picked at the names with his nails.

When he finished, he was sure his parents had, at the very least, the cleanest stones around. He sat with his legs stretched out and his wet, dirty shirt by his side.

He'd hoped a trip to the cemetery would allow him to remember the fond moments he'd shared with his parents. He wanted to reflect on good times that would ease some of the frustration he felt at being banished by Dolly.

The mosquitoes continued buzzing and he repeatedly slapped the back of his neck. He waited for the happy memories to return.

They had died to spite him. They died unwilling to say one kind word to his wife.

He searched harder. One pleasant memory would be enough.

They'd rarely even had a decent dinner together. It was tragic. Ba's was a bland tongue that avoided fragrant spices, Ma couldn't boil an egg, and they always insisted on cooking.

A minute passed like an hour, an hour like a week, and the thought of any stretch of time beyond an hour made his stomach burn.

Each day Calvin wrote a letter to Dolly. Nights he left his room to sit briefly for dinner with Uncle Toh and Ah-Ping. Long after they fell asleep, he lay in bed listening to traffic on the dirt road outside, teenagers zooming past in their Fiats or food-stand operators pedaling their bicycles home.

Mornings he visited his parents' graves, attempting to recover that one happy memory. He stopped by the post office on his way back and express-mailed each letter, tipping the clerks to ensure quick delivery. Arnold called regularly to say Dolly was doing fine, that she was receiving his letters.

Calvin asked if she was reading them.

"She says she is," Arnold said.

Calvin took to sleeping at dawn and waking in mid afternoon. In late afternoon, the road was filled with the bicycles and scooters of those who'd finished the day's work.

One night he heard whispering from the living room: Ah-Ping's hushed demands, Uncle Toh's quiet objections. Then a sigh from Uncle Toh. Footsteps. Then a knock, and Uncle Toh in his doorway.

"How are you?" Uncle Toh asked.

"I'm fine."

His uncle seemed nervous. He leaned against the door-jamb and looked at the floor. "She hears you walking back and forth in here at night. She worries."

"I'm sorry. I'll be quieter."

"She thinks you might kill yourself. She hid all the knives, scissors, rope, aspirin, and masking tape."

"Masking tape?"

Uncle Toh shrugged.

"I'll go out tomorrow night," Calvin said.

"There's a park close by. Twenty minutes from here. You can do all the walking you want there."

"Sure."

"Also."

"Yes?"

"She thinks you don't like her cooking," Uncle Toh said.

"I'm not hungry."

"Every night?"

"It's not her fault," Calvin said.

He continued writing Dolly a letter a day, each asking if he could return. Her responses came every other week in the form of money and a typed note that said, "Dear Husband, Take Care, Best, Dolly."

He began to load his letters with grammatical and spelling errors, hoping that the mistakes would catch her attention and annoy her enough to prompt a more personal response.

"I misse you much," he wrote.

"My heart. Feel break daily.

"I cant't take longer. You make beat my heart.

"I is lost sheep in pasture. You shepard."

Maybe she'd wonder if he'd been struck in the head and worry enough to call. Maybe she actually read his letters.

Finally, he sent Arnold a letter addressed to her.

"Make her open the envelope," he said. "See that her eyes are moving back and forth, down the page. Make sure they don't move too quickly. Imagine you're reading and how fast your eyes would move.

"Then ask her, 'What did you think of dad's descriptions of the banyan trees. What did you think of that three-legged dog?'

"I didn't mention either, so if she says something besides, 'What are you talking about?' make sure she reads it again, out loud, because, what the hey, I put all that effort into writing this thing and she doesn't even read it. *She doesn't even read it.*"

Arnold promised to show Dolly the letter, and the next day, he called back to say that she'd read it and passed the banyan/dog test. She noticed his letters had been badly written lately, and was wondering if he was making some kind of joke at her expense.

"It's not a joke," Calvin said, happy that she'd at least been reading them.

"She's doing fine," Arnold said. "Don't worry. I'm eating with her every other night. She says for you to take care."

"Every other night?"

"But she says that with a lot of feeling," Arnold said.

"Lot of feeling."

"Absolutely."

"And I still can't call her unless I have a terminal disease or need more money?"

"Right," Arnold said.

"What did you think about me getting bit by a dog?" Calvin asked.

"You didn't get bit by a dog."

"I told you last week."

"You didn't."

"You forgot," Calvin said.

"Stop testing me."

"Do you miss me?" Calvin asked.

"Yeah."

"When you say yeah, you sound like you just checked my refrigerator and found nothing."

"What?"

"Nothing," Calvin said. "Listen. After you were born, your mother presented to you baby food with basil leaf towers and lemongrass swirls. I told her babies didn't need basil leaves with their food, but she never listened. All in all, we ate very well for the eighteen years you lived with us, and I thank you for that."

"I'm sorry if I said something stupid," Arnold said.

"You said nothing stupid. Hang up already. This is costing you a fortune."

Arnold hung up, then called back. "You okay?"

"Sure," Calvin said. "I just need some alone time now. Don't call for a while."

Each afternoon the bustle of rush-hour traffic, the steely growls and clanks, came in through the kitchen window.

One day, he called Arnold and left a message on the machine: "You've been a loyal and good son. You accepted all my collect calls without complaint." He couldn't think of anything else to say.

He paced. He took a nap. When rush hour started, he looked through the window.

The scooters and bicycles passed in scattered groups with no lanes to distribute and organize them. Engines whined to catch speed, derailleurs popped, bells tinkled, and tires snapped branches as the riders shifted in their seats.

He followed. He walked along the side of the road and passed schools and hotels. He passed bars and tourist shops that sold miniature Iban longhouses made out of toothpicks. He paused several times to rest while his hands worked sweat from his face.

Eventually, he arrived in a town with an electronics shop at one end and a Subway at the other. A crowd had gathered for dinner and he got in line. He chilled his back against the front window. When the line nudged forward, he stood and left behind a wet, foggy silhouette.

Inside, the store's vents blew cool waves that made him feel lighter.

There was a long glass counter beneath which were sliced tomatoes, bell peppers, and lettuce that gave off a waxy shine. Vinegar and olive oil in bronze bottles. Salt and pepper in sparkling glass shakers. There were sliced bananas and pineapple. Blocks of cheddar and Swiss cheese. The aroma of freshly baked Italian garlic bread.

He felt hungry, wonderfully hungry. Starving. Joyfully lightheaded, and his arms and legs were actually trembling.

"What would you like?" The young Subway employee shined angelic in her golden shirt and visor.

He bought a meatball sub, a tuna, an Italian BMT, a steak

and cheese, a roasted turkey with cheddar, and a Malaysian Special (grilled beef with peanut sauce and onions on wheat).

Then he was at a corner table, tray down, ripping off the wrappers.

He went at it. Drooled over the lettuce. Licked mayonnaise off the sides of his fingers and tore chunks out of sandwiches that had no salt or vinegar because he didn't want to taste anything bitter. He didn't think of Dolly, who he'd always remember at thirty-five, when she'd taken to napping with baby Arnold on the sofa, and hadn't yet learned to look at her husband like he was a bad wedding gift. He didn't think of Arnold, who he once saw at Albertson's actually shopping for himself, carrying a basket full of the Klondike bars his mother so neatly stacked and would continue stacking in her freezer no matter how old he was, or how little room was left. He didn't think of Ma or Ba who, if they could speak from their graves, probably would have just said, "Nice timing coming home."

He gorged. Glutted. He dove facefirst into the bread and meat, coming up only for air. He pushed forward, pushed through, each swallow rapturous, each bite a thrill. He ate. He just ate.

SHORT-STORY AWARD FOR NEW WRITERS
1st-, 2nd-, and 3rd-Place Winners

CHIEH CHIENG, *first-place winner, receives $1200 for his story, "The Exile of Calvin Wu," which begins on page 43, preceded by his profile on page 42.*

AMANDA REA, *second-place winner, receives $500 for "Back Seats."* *She's an MFA in the writing program at the University of California, Irvine, and a recipient of the Deatt Hudson Award for Fiction. She's currently at work on a collection of short stories.*

"Back Seats"

I sleep in my mother's bed, the bed she made each morning for thirty-five years. I sleep between the sheets she folded down at night. I wake up where I was conceived—I've gone exactly nowhere.

C. ABE GAUSTAD, *third-place winner, receives $300 for "Car in the Yard."* *He lives in Knoxville, where he is a PhD student in English at the University of Tennessee. His fiction has recently appeared in* Other Voices *and* New Orleans Review. *When he's not writing stories, he's playing the blues and watching the colors change on the French Broad River.*

"Car in the Yard"

Dora sits cross-legged in front of the television watching a children's show where people dive into muck and filth. It is one of the better things she could watch. She notices me and smiles over her bowl of Froot Loops. If I had gotten up in time I would have made a real breakfast for her.

We invite you to visit **www.glimmertrain.com** *to see a list of the top twenty-five winners and finalists. We thank all entrants for sending in their work.*

Lisa Graley

Those Sears Toughskin bibs were a staple of my childhood. Here I'm pictured with my brother, Michael, on our first bikes on the driveway behind our house. We were—and still are—great companions. In this photo, we're about seven and five years old.

Originally from West Virginia—where she grew up in a town called Sod, attended Marshall University, and then worked four years as a newspaper reporter—Lisa Graley current lives in Lafayette, Louisiana. She has an MFA from McNeese State University in Lake Charles, and a PhD in creative writing from the University of Louisiana at Lafayette, where she now teaches American literature, modern fiction, and creative writing as an adjunct. She tries to spend at least two hours every day writing fiction.

LISA GRALEY
Crossing with Sassafras

goat that a fellow can see through is better than no goat at all. That's how I've come to think of it. With Emma and the children gone, Sassafras will be good company—even though her flying unnerves me. She jigs through the autumn air this morning, lighter than a cloud, her pink udder swaying side to side, flapping against her spindly legs that jerk and propel her past me, sometimes within a hair's breadth. Her hot, grassy breath comes quickly, like she's anxious even, making me believe that if I leaned in close, didn't try to dodge her, she'd tell me a secret, something I want to know. But I haven't found the courage to stand my ground as a man ought, to not flinch when she gallops by so near. The times when I've gathered up my strength, tried to coax her to me, she keeps her distance.

Ever since she showed up, I've been mending her fence, and today, I'm at it again. It's not that I think she'll stay put. I mean, if the fence didn't hold her while she was alive, I can't expect it to keep her ghost. Then why get out and labor and sweat for a lost cause? you will ask. The answer is simple: I want her to know that a goat's ghost is welcome here, can stay as long as there's weeds to trim, bark to gnaw on, tender red bud leaves to chew and swallow and belch up later.

But putting a fence back together is a job for a young man.

I'm not as stout as in the days when I chased her and the others back to the fence every time Emma found them in the garden. With my fingers, I trace the braided, rusty wire between barbs and remember the coarse, white hair I used to find snagged here—evidence of Sassafras passing through. I reach for my handkerchief to soak up the sweat on my head, a trickle under my nose. My fingers streak the handkerchief with gritty rust. I wave this, an orange and white truce flag, at the nanny goat ghost, and for a minute she makes like she will bolt but stays put, wagging her head.

From my shirt pocket, I pull out a long peppermint piece, peel off the sticky wrapper, and try to draw her to me. Sassafras doesn't budge. But at least she's got her hooves on the ground for now. She stares at me like the pasture isn't green enough for her, and it puts me in the notion to just walk away and be done with all her blurry whiteness. But it's that habit she has of looking back over her shoulder, to some distant point in the field, that grips me. It's not the first time she has held me so, spellbound.

"Stop her! Obert—Obert," Emma yells for me. "Stop her. Obert! Where are you?" I've been two hours in the sun-striped stall of the barn, dung to my knees, shoveling flaky manure onto the trailer of my tractor, hearing clump after clump thud in the trailer bed. Despite the handkerchief Emma makes me wear over my face, dust still clots in my nostrils. But even so, I'm happy to take manure dust any day over the soot I breathed in the Buckeye Hollow Mine that one summer working for Emma's father. I choked down that fine coal powder only a month, but I never forgot the gritty dust that laid cover to everything, that burrowed its way under the elastic of your clothes like chiggers and rubbed you raw, that burned in your throat, grated in your teeth, hours after you'd left the hole in the earth.

"Stop her! Stop her, Obert!"

I step around the heaped trailer, and the warm, moist March

air soothes my throat. The fullness of the sun takes away my vision a moment before I catch sight of Sassafras coming toward me, her mouth full of dish rag. Her neck cranes far around, looking back at Emma. All the while the goat walks stiff-leggedly, defiantly, jerking her legs like she's marching. Coming straight for me.

"Obert," Emma says and stops and stamps her feet. Emma. Catch your breath, this, seeing her again. Catch your breath. "Obert! You take this goat on over to Delano Burton's. I don't ever want to see her again. Do you hear me? Do you understand? It's not enough she eats my garden all summer long, but now she's made a meal of my clean wash, too. It's more than a body can stand."

Sassafras hides behind me. I feel her there, warm flank against the back of my legs. Hear her loud breathing, too. Emma drops her hands. "I'm too old to have to be chasing a goat all over creation," she says. "It was different when we were young. Can't you keep her penned in that fence you're always working on?"

Emma swings a poplar switch at her side, and I guess this proves too much for the white nanny. I hear her gagging, feel the ground jar behind me, feel scraping against the back of my boots. I turn to find her lying in the grass, spinning, her head rocking to and fro, eyes large, bright, a choking deep in her throat. The dish rag has vanished. Forcing her jaws, I reach for it, but it's too far gone for me to get a good hold.

"Get my pliers from the garage, from the bucket on the bench—blue-handled ones, long-snouted ones," I yell to Emma. I hold the quivering goat head in my lap, watch her glassy eyes roving to sky to grass to me and around again. How I have hated witnessing it, an impending panic, each and every time. Her milky body stirs, then does not stir; life, still, but escaping out her fragile edges. "It's okay, girl," I tell Sassafras. "It's okay. Don't worry."

"Emma, hurry with the pliers," I whisper under my breath.

"I'm losing her. Emma, hurry, hurry, hurry, hurry. Emma, here to me. Here to me, hurry. As fast as you can. Hurry now."

"Don't worry about supper," I tell Emma. "Just turn off the fire under the beans. The curtains are fine. It's almost dark. Hurry. I *did* lock the doors."

Emma. That single month gone from you was a long time, not knowing when I would be back, if ever I would be. Over at Buckeye, they told me those deep, black tunnels have a way of burying a man's own deep things, of making him forget, deny what's most important to him. You give it all up every time you go down. But I remembered you. I never forgot. Hurry. Your neck, sweet, sweet neck, the delicate nape. Let me touch your neck there, where your hair trails off, swirls, barely wisps. Let me hold my face flush against your face. Do you hear me not breathing? Did you hear the air leave? I'm nearly afraid to touch you. But I do touch you. And cradle your neck in my hand. My face here, Emma, and the soft scent of your skin. I dreamed of your neck in the camps at night. And remembered it and remembered it, remembering it against my face and under my lips, crawling in the tunnels every morning where I could not breathe for the dust. This, all of you. And don't hurry now. Home, to this length of you, against me. Fabric going away, your bare skin. I'm not breathing. Stifled beside you. My face hard pressed against your warm shoulder, I cannot even form my lips to kiss, my mouth, limp, open, against the flesh of your neck. Do you groan? Emma. Emma. I have known you forever. I have never not known you. Emma.

I narrow my eyes to the misty image before me, the nanny goat ghost in the tall, crisp horse weeds that've grown all around and up through the old wooden trailer of my tractor. She sighs, a delicate *mmeheh*, and continues chewing her cud. She scrapes her hoof on the lowered end of the trailer like she's trying to get my attention, like she wants maybe to go for a ride—or like maybe she wishes the children were here,

64

wants to pull them in the trailer the way the other goats did when the children were little. She's about ten feet away, keeping herself out of range of the short-handled hatchet I've been hammering and prying on the fence with. I see the brisk swats of her short tail, batting flies, and hear her steady, slow munching in the quiet of this place. I look around, take a slow sweep of the land, see the horizon wobble a little, move away and come back to me. I wipe my eyes and put the handkerchief back in my pocket.

The earth wobbles again and my head swims. I flip over the tin bucket that hauls my mending tools and sit down. In my deep pockets, the steeple nails scratch my thighs, and I shift my britches so they won't hurt. There's crimson crust on my arm where barbs have caught my skin.

I feel my heart beating fast and hard and close to my throat and wonder if I've overdone it. It's those pills that make me dizzy, the ones the doctor prescribes, pills the children make me promise to take, day in, day out, week after week after week. Before them, I was strong, but now I'm not. They're the same heart pills that took Emma. She told me they made her heart jitter and quake. But I said, "It's something you've been eating, Emma." She said they made her forget things and imagine things that never happened. I said, "Take them, they're for your own good. Take them if they keep you here with me longer." She wanted that, I know as sure as I'm sitting here. But it's been ten years since the pills ate up her heart. Had I been in my right mind, had it not been such a jolt then, maybe I would have started taking them the day she died, the day she stumbled in the garden, panting for air, after we'd picked bushel baskets and buckets of beans and scooted them onto the plywood trailer, its onion-smooth tires sinking deeper in the dirt with each full basket. I remember how she wanted me to take the beans to the house and come back for her with the trailer. She didn't think she could walk. But I knew not to wait and made room for her between the baskets. She wouldn't let me leave any of the beans behind for fear Sassafras would gobble them down. And maybe she would have.

I pull out the handkerchief again and wipe my eyes. Why is Sassafras here—back from the grave? I treated her right. All of us did, even Emma. Did she just get lonesome? Fixing her fence, I haven't made it fifty feet from the barn, and from my bucket seat I survey the line ahead of me, the wire that's been wrenched from termite-whittled posts, some strands now burdened under the weight of a twisted, uprooted willow. It seems an impossible task.

Suddenly Sassafras lifts herself off the ground—like she's a giant bird, yet without wings. She sighs her familiar *mmeheh* and goes back to chewing, suspended there between earth and sky. The grass squeaks in her mouth, and periodically she stops chewing and looks behind her, away over the eerie field like she's expecting someone. I look behind her, too.

Emma rushes, the blue-handled pliers in one hand, the other clutching her blouse at the top to keep it from flying open while she runs. "Here, hurry," she says, crouching beside me.

"You pull the dish rag out," I say. "I'll hold her jaws apart. You pull it out."

"I'm afraid," Emma says. "Maybe I should call Michael. It wouldn't take him long to get here."

"Don't be afraid. Just grab a hold when I open her jaws. Pull gently, not fast."

Sassafras is motionless now, without struggle. The goat's eyes are wide and rolling. I pry, careful not to disjoint her jaws, saliva on my hands, opening, holding open with all my strength. I am shaking. Emma moves her hand, pliers clasped, into the sticky muzzle, further now, and with a good hold, she pulls gently. She pulls slowly, more and more red and white checkers appearing, wet, grassy even. We smell the inside of the goat, a bitter, rotting scent from one of her cavernous stomachs. She gags deep in her throat. They gag, both of them now gagging, and Sassafras coughs, kicks, with the dish rag out, kicks around and whirls herself up, no prisoner, stands coughing, her head down very low and each long, deep cough lifting her off the ground.

"I was afraid we lost her," Emma says and leans against me, and my nose brushes hers, hot tears on her face. Emma. I couldn't have risked missing this, not being here. I couldn't have gone back to Buckeye. It was harder on us this way, with your father's disappointment, and not the money we could have had, the nice cars other men had, the machines that would have made things easier for you in the beginning. I couldn't risk not seeing you again, my eyes filling with the night, the earth swallowing me. I never regretted buying my ticket home, even when I couldn't meet the eyes—eyes so white—of the other miners.

I look at the goat ghost, floating now, about two feet above the ground, above the up-ended trailer, staring past me to the house. I wonder if she's going to fly at me again.

When I hear Emma call that lunch is ready, I swivel on my bucket, my legs stiffening as I try to straighten up. Standing makes my heart beat faster again. She'll probably worry that I'm getting another goat since I've been working on the fence. Will I tell her Sassafras has come back? I picture her watching from the kitchen, scouring dried egg from dishes, muttering to herself, muttering about me out here pouring honey in the pasture. Of course, Sassafras would have nothing to do with the golden, oozing stream—though it used to be a treat for her. When I saw it was so, I wiped the rim of the jar with my forefinger and licked it, screwing on the cap. It takes patience to win a goat. I've always known that.

Inside the house I wash up. The kitchen is empty, and I remember Emma is not here, hasn't been here in a long time. I open a couple of cabinets stocked with the corn, tomatoes, pickles, and peach preserves that Katie's been canning. On the counter she's left a jar of green beans, though she knows

I don't eat them now. Emma could grow them anywhere. Here on the kitchen floor if she wanted. She had a way with them. Slaved to save as many as she could, weeding, and picking, stringing and snapping, washing, her hands in the cool water, fingers sifting, straining them, packing them in quart jars. Thump, thump, thump, the jar on a towel-softened counter, she made them settle tight.

Straight from Buckeye, off the train, with my bag of sooty clothes slung over my shoulder, I've scrubbed myself as much as I could. From outside the screen door on the porch, I watch her. Her elbows bend at right angles over the counter. There's deliberation in all her movements, all of it from memory, having done it so many times before, and the back of her neck, arched now, catches light as she reaches for another jar. The light stays there, a sign. I wasn't made for the dark as some men. I couldn't risk losing this, leaving her, not for any amount of money or her father's good opinion. I wanted every night of my life to be beside her. There wasn't time to waste, not even in the beginning.

How long I watch I don't know. I knock. I'm weak in the knees, all my joints watery. She dries her hands, throwing the dish towel over her shoulder. Backing from the kitchen counter, reluctant to leave, she turns to the door like she doesn't want to be disturbed. But then she says, "You, Obert!" The door swings out far, she fills my arms, just fits there, bouncing up and down, rocking me. Emma, you are lovely. I am not breathing, you are tight around me, tight inside my arms, every muscle straining to be closer, my face brushing your neck. I am not breathing. I am holding you inside my lungs and not breathing. Smile at me. Emma. What? You say, "We have had so many green beans this year."

I warm some leftover potatoes and cream corn from the refrigerator and scoop them onto a plate. The jar of green beans I put on the table, too. While I eat, I run a finger along the cold glass of the jar, the *Ball* lettering. I pick it up to feel the weight. I haven't eaten green beans in ten years. She could make them grow anywhere. But when she died, I tried growing a patch in the garden, just a small one, because I loved them so. Not a single split-seeded vine broke through the earth, and I knew I would never eat them again.

"Obert, will you be having any green beans this evening? There are so many," Emma says. "Did anyone have green beans, where you were, at the camp? When you came out of the mine in the evenings? I put lots of bacon in them, just the way you like them." Her hair is up because I keep going on about how happy I am to look at her lovely neck, to bury my face against her neck. I've been asleep and my clothes are scattered on the floor. The sheets are full of her scents, and above that, on another level, I smell the green beans cooking in the kitchen. My stomach growls. I watch her move around the room in her slip, unpacking my bag, holding my gritty shirt close to her face where the black mixes with her tears.

"Will you go back?" she asks.

"They can't pay me enough, Emma," I say. "I know they're others who like the money, especially when there's none to go around. But I'll see that we get by, I promise. Tell your daddy thanks and all, and not to worry. We'll get by."

I wait for her to say something, but she only smiles, looks at me.

"I've thought about it a lot," I say. "Do you think we could raise goats, Emma?" She squints her eyes like she's trying to better understand me.

"We could sell the milk, butter, cheese," I say. "Probably not much in it, but a little something." I prop myself up on my elbows. "Emma, when I was down there, eating lunch on my back, no such thing as light, I could see them, all white goats, on our hillside, against the green of our hillside. We had them when I was a boy, Emma. Would you like that?" She comes to me across the bed, nestles in my arms, lowering her head on my chest so I can nestle my face against her shoulder. I think of her, my princess in the pasture, white goats all around her flowery skirt.

I've eaten without savoring, have lifted my fork twenty, maybe thirty times without realizing or remembering. The pills make me forget so easily. When I stand, I take the headswim again, blood gushing up there around my brain to the front of my eyes. Suddenly I feel overcome, having the goat ghost on my hands, zinging by my head occasionally, in and out of the house, Emma not around to help me chase the goat back to the pasture. I move to the bedroom, crumple on my bed, atop the covers. My body unfolds easily, smoothes itself out.

I dream but find I am awake with Sassafras sailing about in the room, legs kicking this way and that, her pink udder swinging. Slowly I rise so as not to spook her. She moves like she's not flying but rather running in the air, leaning in as she cuts corners in the room. Come here, girl. Come down from there. We've got to go outside. I reach for her, thinking my hand will go through her, but I catch hold of her slim hind leg, the crook where her skin is thin. She yanks but I don't let go and sense that she is lifting me from the floor, and I am flying, too. She pulls me higher, and when it looks like she will go through the ceiling, I turn loose and fall flat on the bed, almost in a daze.

"Mmeheh," she says, and goes dashing through the wall. I see her then out under the sugar maple, on the ground, looking behind her. Maybe I could call Michael to help me lock her in the barn tonight. But what will he say?

When I finally go back out to catch her again, the evening air is chilly, and the shadows of the hills are long. I pick my way out to the pasture, the goat a few steps ahead of me. I have a cinnamon roll and peppermint pieces for her, and at the pasture I offer them, but she won't come close to me now.

Emma's chased her from the bean vines where she feasted all morning and now she won't forgive me. Neither of them will forgive me.

"She probably consumed fourteen quarts," Emma tells me. "That's fourteen meals when we could have eaten beans this winter, but your goat got them," she says. My eyes follow the direction of her finger, upper end of the garden, the white goat peering through the corn stalks.

"What will you do?" Emma asks. She picks up dirt clods and runs at Sassafras. Yelling, she throws them, and clouds of dust burst all around the goat. Sassafras waits until the very last minute, getting every bite she can, then turns on her heels and runs, cutting in and out of the rows of the garden so tenderly cared for, heading away and then back until she tricks Emma off balance, gets past her and runs to me, like I will save her. But she sees I'm braced to catch her, and when I dive, finding the hard, dry earth smoking in my teeth, she slips through my arms. Emma is over me.

"Get up, get her, Obert. Get that goat."

"Don't run, Emma, you'll scare her—walk slowly." I stalk the goat then, matter-of-factly, with her doing that stiff-legged trot she does, the pink of her behind shining under her raised tail, her looking over her shoulder, back at Emma. "Here, Sassafras, come here, girl. I won't hurt you," I say. "Come here, girl."

Sassafras leads me up the overgrown path. The horseweeds slap my face, and I feel their coarse edges, brown from frost. The air is cool. She stays only a few feet ahead, like she knows I move slower these days. Soon enough, the going gets easier. Through the pine forest where the needles are orange, fiery orange this evening with the sun so low, we go. Around us are the twisted, crackling bushes, twined with dying catbriers. She mounts the hill, a youthful goat. I see her legs pushing off the ground, each strong step to take her higher. And now she leaps over the pushed-down fence, with the same ease she had when it was a good fence. She leads me over the crest to the family cemetery.

"You can't bury her there, Dad," Katie says to me. "What will people say?"

"But she's part of the family," I say. "She has been a friend to me."

"Bury her somewhere else—behind the barn maybe," Michael says.

"It's a private cemetery," I say. "No one comes here, no one will ever know there's a goat buried here. It's not like I'm going to buy a monument for her or anything. I'll just carve her name on a rock. She's been with me so long and given me reason to get up in the mornings after your mother died, after I got Emma home in the trailer that day, and before I could even lift her from it, when she could not catch her breath."

"Breathe slowly," I said, "please, hold on, breathe slowly now." Her eyes were wide. "I don't want to leave you, I don't want you to leave. Please, breathe slowly, in and out, in and out." My hand is under her head, cradling her neck, wet and hot. "Hold on, I'll call the children. Hold on, they'll hurry—they will be here, we'll get you to the hospital. Hold on, Emma, breathe, I am with you, don't be afraid, please, breathe, breathe, please, please, please."

Her eyes are far brighter than in life, wide open, taking in everything, or maybe nothing. "Emma, please, you're not breathing. You're not trying. Please breathe."

"Let me stay with her," I tell the ambulance driver. "She's scared—please save her, give her back to me, please. Emma. Let me hold her hand."

"Take my hand, Dad, while we walk there," Katie says. "Mom will rest there. She'll be okay, happy on this hill, near the pasture, not too far from the garden she loved."

"It's not an easy walk," I say. I've walked it hundreds of times, checking the fence, mending the gaps, but it seems like today I can't bring myself to walk it. They carry her slowly, steadily. Sometimes they slide in the red mud. Their arms are tense. They don't want to drop her. Seems like my feet are going without my moving them. At the graveside, they would leave the coffin on top like that, wait for me to leave, to turn my head. It doesn't make sense to me. Seeing a thing done means seeing it done.

"I'm not leaving," I tell them. "Be done with it, boys."

"Dad, walk back with me."

"You don't understand," I say. "Let me be." It doesn't take long, not long at all, once they've lowered her into the earth. Their shoulders and elbows bending, they send the red dirt through the air. It thuds below at first but then just falls softly and silently and finally they're ready to leave. They think I'm going to be a hard case. But I'm not. I just want to be left alone with her. "Go on home," I say, "I want to be alone. Come back for me if it makes you feel better, just leave me here a while. I'll be ready when you come back."

I don't want to be alone, please, Emma. After that first month away, I never left again. I could not. You know that. We were never apart again.

"I will not leave you," I tell her, the bean juice sticky on my chin. "You never leave me either, you hear, Emma."

"Why would I?" she says, snuggling close. "You're my world."

The shoveling done, men gone, I can't wait for anyone to come back, and I leave the mound, the place they've put Emma. At the fence, on her side for once, Sassafras—she knows. Through the fence I touch her pink nose.

"Mmeheh," she says.

"Mmeheh," I repeat. I walk up a ways to the gate and enter the pasture to be with her. We walk back together, not wanting to go home but not wanting to go anywhere else either. She picks at a leaf here and there, but that's all. Like me, she's not hungry.

She leads me past the cemetery, high up on Mark's Knob, to that steep place. I know she's going to fly. I know it. I want to catch her at that moment, to stop her before she leaps up. I want to bring her home with me, tie her to the poplar in the yard till I get the fence fixed, keep her from going away from me again. I crawl on my hands and knees now and feel the earth under my palms. I scoot toward the edge where she pauses to look back over her shoulder—but not at me, past me.

"Mmeheh," she says. Her cry is urgent. She stares past me but I see nothing unusual. I reach for her as far as—reach—all of me stretching—another inch or—all my—this—is all—to grab hold of her, to clutch her to myself. My fingers find her coarse hair, joint of her hind leg, almost within my grip. All the way. Emma, I have her. She's lifting off the ground. I have her, I will, I have her this time. But my hand is slipping, I can't hold on much longer, she is, I am, slipping, and I lose hold, fall, am rolling, down the hill. I go down, sliding and rolling, with the earth and leaves blurry fast in front of my face. Until it all stops, and my body curls inward to the burning pain.

I look up at the sky, see the ghost goat hovering above the persimmon trees. Can't she see I want her to stay, that there's room here for her? I stand up, my head reeling. Sassafras floats out of sight, leaving me behind. I brush off my clothes and head toward home. Emma will be worried, will have supper on the table waiting for me, maybe even her green beans this evening.

"Emma," I say, entering. "I'm home." But there's no answer and I guess she's running late. I don't know when she'll be home, and I figure I'll have to cook the beans for us. I wash my hands and pop open the lid of the jar with a can opener. Dump them into a pot on the stove and turn the fire on. I wash the day's dirty dishes while they heat up. I'm tired and I wish Emma would get home soon to eat supper with me. It's not like her to be gone anywhere this late.

Through the window I see Sassafras perched in the sugar maple—aglow. I can't tell if she's standing on a branch or just floating at the moment. It's too much for an old man like me, having a crazy goat who doesn't know whether she's beast or bird. I keep my eye on her, and when the beans are ready, I lift about five tablespoons into a dish for me and three into a dish

74

for Sassafras. I set hers in the floor, trying to lure her into the house while Emma isn't here. I put the lid on the pot so the beans will stay warm till Emma gets back.

Back through the dark house I go with my beans. In the bedroom, Sassafras surprises me, having come through the wall. Her glow lights the room. Emma will not be happy about having a goat in the house, but Sassafras needs a place to stay until I can get the fence finished. I'll just have to explain it to her. On the bed, I pull the blankets over me and lie back. With my fingers, I eat the beans. They're fine in the way they're always fine, and I keep nibbling at them, trying to savor each one, figuring they'll tide me over till Emma's home for supper.

The dish is warm, is heaped high, green beans and a strand or two of bacon threading through, on my bare chest, warm, the dish, when you feed them to me, one at a time, with your fingers, picking one and putting it in my mouth, watching my face, waiting till I swallow before reaching for another, every green bean on the plate this way, and occasionally, one wrapped with a shred of limp bacon, until the dish is empty and there's just the juice which you drain into my mouth, down my chin, across my chest, that you kiss clean.

Sassafras never eats them hot because they burn her mouth. But she likes them cold, cooked or raw. When she takes sick, I bring some candy to the stall where she lies, thinking it might help her. She eats it all from my hand, careful, as she always has been, not to bite my fingers. She eats everything I bring today but tomorrow she won't. She doesn't stand now. Her bowels aren't moving. She coughs. When she begins the loud, gut-wrenching bellows, I know what will have to happen.

"Maybe we can call a doctor," Katie says. "Or Delano Burton. He'll know what to do."

"She's very old," I say. "She's suffering. I'll hitch up the trailer, carry her back on the hill, and we'll put an end to it."

Emma's been gone four years, so it's the children, Michael and Katie, who help me lift her, mmehehing, mmehehing, to the trailer.

"You ride back here with her," I tell them. But they don't want to. They are grown now.

"I can't do it, Dad," Katie says. "I can't."

"I can't either," Michael says. "Shouldn't we call the vet? Get him to give her a shot?"

"One of you will have to drive the tractor then," I say, "and I'll ride with her. You can leave before I do it." Emma would have stayed with me, would have known what it required—and would have been my help.

Beside the grave, just at the boundary of the cemetery, a place where no one else would want to be buried, I give her peppermint. The children leave, don't even look back over their shoulders. I watch them as long as I can and turn back to Sassafras who drops the peppermint from her mouth. My jaws are so tight they hurt, my throat knotted like I might vomit. I pet her head, run my hand gently on her floppy ears. "Mmeheh." She is swollen and cannot stand. She cries out at all hours. She is fourteen, a ripe age for a goat, one we thought would die a day old. When the mother died, Emma fed her formula with a nippled RC bottle, named her Sassafras, and the tiny kid ate, punching her nose at the nipple, milk bubbles foaming at the sides of her mouth, her tail spinning, spinning. You cradle her as one of your own, Emma, as me even, soothing her head, your fingers soft and strong, scent of green beans on them, taste of them, passing over my lips, the edges of my teeth.

The gun is nothing but weight and cold. It has always seemed so to me. You never asked me to do it, would never have, no matter how many beans Sassafras ate. But there isn't a choice now. She won't get up again. I've seen it too many times with all the other goats. You have been gone from me three long years. You were my strength. Just to have you again, Emma. That last day, losing you.

I aim, but not I, someone else, at her head, not her head, there, just a target, I pretend, and squeeze. One shot. Then a second. They shouldn't let me do it. I'm no good with a gun, have never been, have made a mess of it. And am too old. I don't have the stomach. Didn't even as a young man. They haul that miner up, pulling him out on a rail cart, mangled. He's one of the lucky ones, someone says. At least they got his body. I don't know him, so it isn't that. You just never know when you go under if you'll see daylight again, or the other things that light your life. His wife is soaked in the rain, a scarf pasted to her head. When she sees his body, so pale and broken, she reaches, knees going, her head bowed, her neck, a flash of your head bent, the back of your neck catching light, while you string beans. I couldn't go down there again. I walked away the same hour and bought my ticket home. Some men get over it or get used to it, your daddy told me. But I thought my train to you would never come.

My skin is cool, damp from sweat tonight. The cold dish lies empty on my chest. It's dark all around. Momentarily, I close my eyes, stilling myself, quieting my heart, while I wait. When I open my eyes, Sassafras is on her way down again, bright as day, pulling a trailer out of the sky. She looks behind her, away off in the distance toward the bean patch where Emma stands, waving, yelling that it's supper time. Sassafras comes closer and closer, trotting her stiff-legged gait, finally swinging the trailer down within reach. When she halts in front of me, I hoist myself up and climb aboard to go.

Cate McGowan

*Probably tired (I still weep when I'm tired), I remember sobbing before
my bath—note the shower cap. At some point, in the midst of my
wailing, my mother interrupted, saying,* Wait, let me get my camera!

*"How weird," I thought. "Mom wants to snap shots of me while
I'm freaking out." It caught me off guard. And though I was
bewildered by this odd new behavior of my mother's, I relented,
with the one condition that she couldn't shoot me* nekkid.
*My mother clicked away, as I buried my face in the towel, wiped
my wet eyes. A future of similar negotiations was before me.*

Cate McGowan is in her second year in the MFA brief-residency program at
Spalding University. She lives in Atlanta where she continues to write and
learn to fly with her boyfriend and three cats, Gracie, Floyd, and Bocephus.

CATE McGOWAN
Arm, Clean Off

*T*he irrigation machine took it, slashed his arm off, a thick gash and a click of bones as it sliced right through. He'd dropped the wrench, reached into the engine to retrieve it. His dad had always said not to, but who would know? No one was around. The alfalfa grass swayed with a rushing sound, skeins of dry waves dancing in rhythm to pulsing water. The long arm of the irrigation machine spewed water; its wheels rolled by him like a slow locomotive, oblivious to his crisis, a grinding mechanism, craning over a fourteen year old.

It had all happened in a split second. He'd been distracted by a spotted hawk swooping down on a squirrel; he was stretching his arm for that wrench he dropped, just a little further, just there at the tips of his fingers. He'd looked down from the hawk in time to watch the fan chew his arm off, just like in the movies, like it was happening to someone else; no time to snatch it out of harm's way. The engine's fan had cut off his left arm, clean off. Just above the elbow.

He dove off the top of the engine head first, into the wet field, green clumps swallowing him up. Blood was gushing now. He licked the salty corners of his mouth, stared up into the navy sky above, and saw red on the plants where he'd fallen through. He lay back, thinking through the blood to shape a plan. He thought, I'm not dead yet, no, no, that thump under my eyes is my heart. Down the slope, he could see the farmhouse and the creek. He was alone—it was Saturday morning. He'd been left to work; they were all in town shopping. No one could hear him call. The field was empty— only the fierce, excited din of birds and bugs from all sides, the occasional bark of a dog from a distant farm.

He could lie there or get up, he thought, blinking his eyes to dispel the dizziness. I'll lie here a second. I'll catch my breath, he thought. That blue sky overhead, the clouds all crisscrossing, is a big stadium, a broad net. Other people have emergencies, everybody does. Everybody takes a look up at the sky sometime, faces it. He thought of those people in other places, lying in rocky soil, watching the same sky. Beautiful girls pouting in parks, kids homesick at camp. Flat on their backs.

The cut decided on a dull throb, which droned in tempo to his pulse—one-and-two-and, one-and-two-and… He reached his right hand over and felt something fleshy. His sleeve was torn. Mom wouldn't be too happy about that. He felt something sticky over by his knee as he tried to sit up. It was his arm, the one that was cut off. He clutched it, covered in blood, to his chest, then set it down gingerly.

He'd seen tourniquets done in lots of Westerns. *A tourniquet'll save your life,* his dad had said. The belt came off easy, even with one arm. He unbuckled it, slid it through his belt loops in one motion. Getting the belt around his arm would be the hard part. He held the leather in his teeth and lay down to wiggle the new stub through the loop, then grabbed the end with his good hand and cinched it, then gripped it in his teeth again. Groping around, he found a thick twig left over from trees they'd felled last year, stuck it in the buckle, twisted it, tightened it over his arm, fastened it with the bandanna from around his neck. Blood was everywhere; he swiped his gooey hand along the leg of his jeans.

He'd walk. With his arm. The field was spinning with the irrigation. Water was in his boots now. The dark, rich soil made an oozing, bubbling sound as he stepped. The tractor was a good ways off, maybe a half mile. Dad didn't like him to drive, but he'd have to now. He could feel his key ring jingle in his pocket as he walked. Up the hill, he knew he could make it, up the small hill through the trees. Dad had always parked the John Deere under a tree, by the road, so it wouldn't get wet. *Out of reach of that damned machine*, his dad said. Now it was out of his reach.

His cut-off arm was dead weight, like a football cradled there, nestling in the crook of his right arm; he touched his fingers there. How strange—it's asleep, yes, it needs some rest for the long journey, he thought. No sensations; it's waiting, waiting, tingling. One foot, then the other.

He thought he was probably losing lots of blood now. Water from the machine had collected on his eyebrows, trickled into his eyes. He couldn't chance swiping his good hand across his face, losing the precious package. It might roll down the hill. With the thought of his arm rolling down the hill, he remembered "The Poor Meatball Song" he'd learned at camp. "It rolled off the table and out through the door." Dad is gonna be mad, he thought, I left that machine going full throttle.

The day burst with changing light, and, as he walked in and out of shadows, it was all purple and pink. The morning sun reflected in the wet grass like shattered glass, and the field looked like an ocean, though he'd never seen one. Everything moved in the breeze. Cloud shadows passed back and forth. The trees in the distance were dancing. The grass bent all together, and there was a zigzagging pattern across the field where a groundhog was running. Think through this, he thought, ignore the throb. Were all these sights just delirium? No, he was sure he was walking diagonally up the long, sloping tract.

I am walking toward help, he thought, with the grass moving like water, and there's no one. Got to reach the pine woods. Two fields down a ways was the house, waiting and empty, and off to his left, hidden by trees, almost out of sight, was the John Deere for which his dad had outbid everyone at the co-op. Up through the clearing he stumbled, leaving the field, stepping between two crabapple trees. He found the path easily.

He made it to the tractor. A crow—no, two—perched on the steering wheel. They took off only as he approached, reluctantly, with a brush of wings. "You ain't gettin' my arm!" He screamed after them, remembering the times he'd seen crows pecking roadkill.

It was a hard start, the tractor, especially when it was cold. Always had been. But the pine trees hadn't shaded it all morning, so he knew it was warm enough. He gripped his cut-off arm on the seat between his knees, twisted his tourniquet, tightened it a little, then gunned the engine. A breeze, tinged with the sweet smell of fresh manure, blew in from Potter's. That's it, that's where he'd go.

He U-turned, easy enough with one arm, but the spots in his eyes were big. Everything was getting foggy, zooming inwards. No, he blinked hard, I'm not going to pass out. And before he could blink again, there was a pine looming large in front of him. He'd pulled the clutch out too late, the tractor had stalled, and the bumper'd wedged between a stump and a tree. He turned the key a few times—it was flooded, he knew it.

He pried his arm from between his knees, the fingers dangling lifeless, and he saw dirt under the nails and a hangnail and a white, full crescent under the thumbnail. He headed for the creek: his dad kept a truck for towing logs down there in the ravine, off the old farm road. Only a few more steps, he thought. I wonder if I'm leaving a trail of blood.

A flurry of gnats swarmed in his face, around his wound. He

ducked wildly to avoid them. A breathless symphony of cicadas and bullfrogs played on all sides. Raw, melancholy calls of crows—*caw, caw, caw*—sang to him. A powerful heat rose from the ground, rushed up his body, into his face, down to the gash. The gnats seemed to disappear, but maybe he wasn't noticing them anymore. He thought, That sky looks bleached out, that sickle moon looks so comfortable resting there on top of tree points, like a broken egg in a nest. Down the ravine he stumbled, the clay soil rucking up behind him. The bottle-green water trickled over pebbles and rocks in the stream.

The truck—*She's a good ol' truck*, Dad always said—there she was. Down with the clutch, in with the key—it was getting hard to keep his eyes open now, he had to think in steps. The truck fired and started right up. His arm was on the seat beside him. Did I put it there? he thought. He twisted the tourniquet again, then pulled the truck into gear with his only good hand. Only one turn to Potter's.

Out the road, he turned left, this time avoiding trees. Now the pines were all canopies for him, shielding him from the sun, like a tent or all those awnings they have in big cities. He was so thirsty. He'd find help.

The closest farm, Potter's. Just around the bend. He pulled up to their barn, the biggest in the county, then slid off the seat to the ground, reached up and honked the horn. He couldn't cry out, his throat was too dry, the beating behind his eyelids had started to slow down.

Mrs. Potter appeared out of nowhere; her long legs in work pants, an apron around her waist, she stood there, her mouth a big O. She was hollering for her husband, for everybody. I don't remember the truck being red, he thought, as he watched Mr. Potter run over with two farm hands. They crossed the yard in a hurry.

"Can I have a glass of water, please?" was the first thing he said. He hung his head, shielding his eyes from the slanting sun. Mr. Potter had on mismatched boots.

"My arm's in there." He pointed to his arm sitting alone and dirty on the truck seat, then turned to see Mr. Potter undo his own belt, yank it from his pants like a whip, and make a new tourniquet.

"This should help, son." Mr. Potter spun around to face his wife and spoke in a hushed tone. "Now, put that arm on ice and call 911. Let's get a blanket, and, for God's sake, call his parents." Mr. Potter turned back, twisted the tourniquet tight, and said, "We're gonna carry you to the porch, okay? Outta the sun. You'll be okay. I bet you get to ride in a helicopter or somethin'." Mrs. Potter whisked the arm away. Two more Mexican workers ran from the barn, and they all fetched him up like a hog-tied goat. Someone was calling the hospital from inside the house. He'd see his arm again. Maybe they could put it back on; they have the technology, he thought.

In a moment, Mrs. Potter was back beside him, her apron off now. "There're your parents, there they come right now, right on down the road." She pointed to his mom's car, broken taillights braking on the curve, turning off the main road. Mrs. Potter had little glistening beads of sweat on her upper lip, in the fur there, when she held the glass for him to drink.

From the porch, he saw a cumulus cloud far in the west, forming a big hand, with the forefinger pointing down, like the famous picture he'd seen somewhere of God reaching to Adam. He knew he'd have to tell his parents he messed up. They were going to be really mad. He'd tell them, Don't cry, Mom. Dad, you stop your crying.

POETRY OPEN
1st-, 2nd-, and 3rd-Place Winners

First-place winner: ZOË GRIFFITH-JONES
"Who Am I to Say"

Zoë Griffith-Jones receives $500 for her first-place poem, which appears on page 87, preceded by her profile on page 86.

Second-place winner: PATRICIA MURPHY
"Inevitable Flow"

Patricia Murphy earned Bachelor's degrees in English and French literature from Miami University, and an MFA in Poetry from Arizona State University, where she currently teaches writing. Her poems have appeared in numerous journals, including the Iowa Review, Quarterly West, *and* American Poetry Review. *She has received awards from the Associated Writing Programs and the Academy of American Poets.*

Third-place winner: JENNIFER MELEANA HEE
"Genealogy"

Jennifer Meleana Hee is the only English teacher at Iolani School with a tongue piercing. She lives in Honolulu and is both a nationally certified Turbo Kickbox instructor and Harvard graduate. This is the first poetry contest she has entered as a grown-up.

We invite you to our website (www.glimmertrain.com) to see a listing of the top twenty-five winners and finalists, and our online submission procedures. We thank all entrants for sending in their work.

Zoë Griffith-Jones

In March 1957, this photo traveled from California to England,
and only recently returned. On the back, in my mother's handwriting,
it says, "Zoë in her new smocked frock. Note Ti plant in foreground."
I have no idea why the Ti plant was newsworthy.

Zoë Griffith-Jones's writing career has encompassed journalism, advertising, personal essays, and poetry. Her work has appeared in *Tiny Lights*. She is currently a private investigator in Sonoma County, California, and writes about the people she encounters, who are, indeed, stranger than fiction. This is her first published poem.

ZOË GRIFFITH-JONES
Who Am I to Say

> Regrets, I've had a few,
> but then again, too few to mention.
> — Frank Sinatra

Well bully for you, Frankie.
If you're keeping track, I think you
should regret recording "My Way,"
but who am I to say—my own catalog is
endless:
those roads to success that beckoned
but seemed too long a trek,
the bridges burned in fiery rages,
the rash decisions, the bitter words I could not suck
back into my throat where they might have stuck, straining
to escape, but would not have stung those in their way;
the second child I did not bear, who in my mind still
adores me unreservedly, but who am I to say—she might
have grown
to love the needle more, the sting of the serpent's tooth.
Who am I to say that the missteps, the wrong turns,
the bright lights that lured and burned and seared my heart
leaving scars of regret—who am I to say they didn't,
in the end,
make me whole.

Laurence de Looze

Taking my first call.

Laurence de Looze has published fiction, essays, and translations in the *Antioch Review*, the *Ontario Review*, *Carolina Quarterly*, *Northwest Review*, *Exile*, *MSS*, and other journals. A native of Oregon, he now lives and teaches in Canada.

LAURENCE DE LOOZE

Berlin Station

*O*n *Saturday, April 3, 1977, when the* Junta *in Argentina was at its height, seven political prisoners escaped buck naked into the countryside less than an hour from the city of Buenos Aires. They had been held in a converted chalet in a little village known for its vacation cottages. In their last couple of weeks of detention the detainees noticed that the guards had taken to playing cards all night downstairs in the furnace room, leaving the prisoners virtually unguarded. They calculated that if they broke out in the middle of the night, no one would be the wiser until dawn.*

That night those seven succeeded in sabotaging the doors of their cells. They had been tipped off that the front door of the house was not locked. Once outside, they fled naked through the fields for hours. When they came upon a little store, they broke in and called one of their fathers to come pick them up. After that they were hidden in a farmhouse for several months until they could be smuggled out of the country. For their protection, not even their families were told they were alive.

Back at the chalet, the breakout was discovered around dawn the next morning. All hell broke loose then. The prisoners that remained were transferred that very afternoon and were never seen again. Were some drugged and flown out over the Atlantic where they were tossed from the plane—one of the famous aviones sin puertas *(planes without doors)? Or were they all just taken to a field and shot?*

Glimmer Train Stories, Issue 47, Summer 2003
©*2003 Laurence de Looze*

No one ever knew. The only thing that was for sure was that freedom for the seven escapees was a death warrant for the others...

The detention center (1)

There was the little row of cells, and El Bajito, the guard who was nice, and El Macho, who was not, and Pablo in the next cell, as well as Flaquito, who shared Octavio's cell. There were the blindfolds on their eyes and the screams late at night from the room downstairs, and the fading hope that any of them would ever make it out. There were the images that flashed on the walls of his eyelids (Octavio never quite knew whether to try to keep his eyes open or closed under the blindfold): of the old neighborhood with its little shops and newspaper stand, of his first guitar, of Yolanda. There were distant Sunday mornings when, as a boy, he had played soccer with his father. And there was the sad realization that before being abducted you never appreciated how exquisite and lovely little things like running out of butter, or missing a bus, or arriving home tired from work could be.

I'm lucky in one thing, Octavio told himself sometimes— to the extent that anything about being sequestered was lucky: Flaquito is smart, and you can talk to him. Octavio told him everything. About Yolanda, and about his father Tudor escaping from Rumania in the 1930s; about the clandestine concerts his group had played in coffee houses around Buenos Aires. He even told Flaquito about the one time he had been unfaithful to Yolanda. Just one night, a night without any real importance, but as a prisoner Octavio had plenty of time to think about things that had no importance. He had plenty of time to think about everything. You couldn't do much else blindfolded. Octavio felt he had betrayed Yolanda. It had been after a concert, with a young woman he had never seen before. Or after. She had been watching him while he played. They ducked into a room, a kind of warehouse, above the café. He never got around to asking her name.

There were three cells in a row, and Octavio's was the first of the three. The detention center had once been somebody's vacation home. There was an upstairs and a downstairs, a front door and a back one, and these things all had their special meanings now that it was used for prisoners. Octavio guessed there had originally been three, maybe four bedrooms. His and Flaquito's cell was the smallest of the ones carved out of the bedrooms on the main floor. Pablo and José were in the cell beside them. When the death squads first kidnapped you, they marched you up to the front door, like you were going on vacation. You quickly learned that if they took someone down to the one in the basement, just off the furnace room, it meant they were "transferring" him. "Transferring" was a euphemism for being taken out and executed. They transferred a few prisoners every month, just to shake things up.

Upstairs and downstairs. Women prisoners were kept downstairs, the men upstairs. No wonder the guards liked it better downstairs, the prisoners joked. After all, the men were kept naked, except when there was some kind of bigshot coming or you were being transferred. It was strange that they put clothes back on you when they wanted to kill you. The women were probably kept naked too, they reckoned. He knew every attractive woman got raped. And he had always thought Yolanda was beautiful.

Tudor (1)

Tudor Podulu had always been a religious man and a fatalist. In the 1920s, as a child in Rumania, Tudor had wanted to be a rabbi, but that had all been changed by his mother's decision. He ended up in Argentina working in dry goods instead of in Bucharest working in a temple. He believed this was his fate and did not complain.

In 1938 Tudor's mother sensed the drift of things to come and insisted he leave the country. He was seventeen at the time. At first Tudor refused. Then he agreed, on the condition that he get to go to Italy. There was a naval school in Naples that took Jews. Tudor wanted to see the world.

It was only after Tudor was well on his way that he realized the train was not going to Italy. It slowly curved North instead of South. When he showed his ticket to the conductor, the man laughed.

"Italy?" the trainman shouted above the clack of the wheels. "You're headed to Holland, not Italy!"

When the train stopped at the German border, Tudor briefly considered jumping off. In retrospect, he was glad he hadn't done so. From Holland he went to England and from England he had been sent to Argentina, he never quite knew why. Maybe because, being Rumanian, it would be easier for him to learn Spanish than English. After World War II was over, he considered moving to Palestine, but never did.

When Israel was founded, Tudor had a bride sent over from the promised land. She got off the ship in Buenos Aires with nothing but her suitcases and a photo Tudor had sent of himself, so she would be able to recognize him. He also had one of her. Octavio often imagined them searching through the crowds for each other, holding up their pictures before them like magic icons.

When they found each other on the wharf, Tudor chalked it up to God's will. He had done quite well for himself and had a new house to bring his bride home to.

"Argentina," Tudor always said, "is a fine country to have ended up in. It is a blessed country!"

Renate

In prison, Octavio thought more about his mother than his father. Tudor had so much faith, it was amazing. Octavio's mother, Renate, did not. Her motto was that you could never be too sure.

As a little boy Octavio thought his mother was the most beautiful woman in the world. He told her once when he was five that he wanted to die when she did. He didn't want to live a day longer than her. Strange, in prison he felt almost guilty that he might be the one to die first. That had never entered his mind before.

Worry had made Renate age. She looked older than Tudor (actually she was eight years younger) and she wore her hair back in a bun. Renate had been born in a village north of Vercelli, near the German border. They sent her to Palestine as a refugee when the pogroms began, but not before her two brothers and father were shut into a burning shed in 1939. Renate and her mother fled into a forest, where they stayed for two days before coming out. This happened even though the village priest had promised his protection to the Jews.

Music

Renate's mother had been a music teacher, and Renate attended the conservatory in Tel Aviv. Later, in Buenos Aires she gave occasional piano lessons. She sang too.

She used to sing Octavio to sleep, placing herself at the door of his room after she turned the light out. The melodies expanded in the dark: the sound flowing out from her black, flat silhouette. The songs came back to Octavio in the detention center: Schubert lieder, settings of Victor Hugo by Gabriel Fauré, snippets from arias. It was almost like putting on a record in his head; he got so he could choose a song or even a particular moment in a song and mentally start the needle wherever he wanted.

Renate encouraged Octavio to be a musician. Tudor had a more practical approach. "Learn music but study law!" he always said. Tudor repeated this statement all of Octavio's life, even though Tudor himself was a reasonably good violinist. It meant: music is good for the soul, but don't make a career of it.

When Octavio switched from classical music to folk, it made his mother sad. But what worried her more was when his songs started to get political. She chalked that change up to Yolanda. Renate had a habit of touching her bun when she was worried. By 1975 she adjusted it constantly on the nights Octavio played the student cafés.

The Seder

Octavio never liked the food at Seder dinners. He was always starving, and as they ate the unleavened bread and sang songs and sampled the sweet along with the bitter (sweet because life was sweet, bitter because life was bitter, too), he always craved something more substantial. He was too hungry to concentrate on the biblical stories, and until he was twelve he was not allowed to participate in the glasses of wine (the first time he did he, of course, got so drunk he couldn't make it through the meal). The chants, the history of the Jewish people, the sufferings, the Jews saved by the angel who passed over…

Also the tale of Tudor's escape from Rumania. Each year at the Seder Octavio's father told the story of how his mother had sent him out of Rumania in 1938. As a young boy Octavio just assumed the story was part of the standard ritual in all Jewish households. He was nearly ten before he realized there was a difference between the biblical texts and his father's tale.

"Prison is like a Seder," he whispered to Flaquito one day while they were eating what passed for dinner, "except they give you even less food, and it's worse."

Flaquito thought this was so funny he only stopped giggling when he heard the steps of a guard outside the cell. The little slit in the door opened and an eye peered in.

It was El Bajito, Octavio could tell (you could always make out a few details around the edge of your blindfold—it was a matter of positioning your head). What El Bajito saw was the two of them eating in silence. In prison you learned to make fast changes. Octavio had long since figured out how to handle

El Bajito. The more innocuous you made yourself, the less he applied the rules. Octavio sometimes thought El Bajito wanted to wish things away, wish away the whole clandestine center with its rooms remodeled into cells. Octavio suspected El Bajito was a conscript who felt he had been dealt a hand almost as lousy as the prisoners.

The voyage

Octavio had heard his father's story each year for as long as he could remember. The angel had passed Tudor over. When Octavio was little he listened in awed silence to their father. He knew what was coming next—after the part about the train being headed toward Holland.

"It was Providence," Tudor would say (deep nods from the elders; if the rabbi was present he mumbled a blessing). "My mother knew what was in store for the Jews. Bless their souls, they all perished."

Over time Octavio learned what it meant for people to perish. In 1968, when he was fourteen, the family took a boat to Europe. They went first to England, then across to Holland. The family repeated Tudor's train trip in reverse: Octavio retained the image of an endless landscape pulled sideways for several days and nights as the train lumbered East. From Rumania Tudor dragged them all to Poland and the death camp where the rest of his family had been sent.

"It was here," he said sadly, "here that they perished." Octavio stared at the empty rooms where terrible things had taken place. He tried to imagine that the cells had once housed innocent victims, that members of his own family had passed through those rooms: that they had cried out in pain. He had the image of a terrible world—a kind of parallel world be-hind the stone walls—in which people had been caught like flies in honey. He stared at the cells and wondered what would happen if somehow that parallel time suddenly punched through the thick walls. Which world would triumph?

The whole trip lasted six months, and Octavio lost a year of school as a result. After that Octavio listened much more intently to the comments about how the family perished.

Still, the part of the story that had the most effect on Octavio was when his father had to change trains in Berlin.

The cello (1)

Octavio never knew who first decided he should study music. It was as though it had been understood from the time of his birth, an unquestioned part of life, like eating or breathing or brushing your teeth. Jews loved to make music, he had been told that often enough. Back in his father's village, almost everyone learned to play one instrument or another. And because of his mother, there were often musicians around their house. Some came to play quartets, some came for a free meal. Their musician friend Hugo always came in the hopes that he might also steal a kiss from Renate while they were in the kitchen. It was Hugo who decided Octavio was to study cello.

It happened so fast that what Octavio remembered most of all was his confusion that night, when his mother pulled him out of bed in the wee hours and padded him down the stairs to the living room. Octavio was not more than five at the time.

Tudor was sitting there with Hugo—*Maestro Hugo!* they called him—in big armchairs in front of a roaring fire.

Hugo was a huge, barrel-chested man, also from Central Europe. Hungarian, maybe, or Czech. Hugo swatted Octavio as he came in—for good measure.

"Let me see your hands, boy!" Hugo shouted as Octavio passed.

Octavio was a little scared. For protection he stationed himself beside his father's legs.

"The hands! The hands!" Hugo shouted again.

Tudor laughed and nudged Octavio forward.

"Hold up your hands, dear," Octavio's mother called gently from behind Hugo's chair.

When Octavio took a step forward he slipped and almost fell. But he caught himself.

He saw Hugo gesturing to him and stepped forward bravely. Hugo stood up, and his huge frame all but blotted out the light from the fire.

"These haaannds!" Hugo said slowly in a deep *basso* voice.

Octavio held out his hands.

Hugo took them in his own and turned them over several times.

Then he bowed ceremoniously to Octavio's mother. "Madame, your son has the hands of a cellist." His eyes twinkled. Then he shrugged and added, "Or if not a cellist, then a criminal."

And with that the matter was decided. The next morning his parents told him he was going to begin the cello, and they had made arrangements to have a miniature one sent from Germany. Weeks later a crate arrived, and Renate had it set in the middle of the living room until Tudor got home. Then Tudor pried off the top with a crowbar.

The crate was filled with packing material. When they got to the center, however, Octavio saw it: wrapped in cloth, lying prone, a kind of mummy in eternal sleep—his first cello.

Tudor slowly lifted it out and unwound the binding. What emerged was a delicate body—like that of a young girl. It was like a violin, only bigger—almost the same height as Octavio. Octavio knew instantly he had a new companion, a silent friend.

That evening Hugo came over with a big bottle of champagne. He set up the bridge and tuned the strings. Then he put the instrument under his enormous chin and played it like a fiddle, making everyone laugh. Finally he pulled out the peg and stood the cello before Octavio.

"Take it," he shouted. Octavio put his arm around its neck.

Hugo uncorked the champagne and everyone drank. Even

Octavio had a sip of the bitter drink from his mother's glass. After the champagne the adults had cognac, and after that Hugo and Renate sang duets.

Many years later it occurred to Octavio that the three adults must have been riotously drunk by the end of the evening. One day in his cell, Octavio started thinking about Hugo and the evenings of music and drink, and it occurred to him that maybe his mother had been in love with the huge man.

The Cello (2)

In any event that drunken night decided matters (Tudor would have called it fate), and so began a ten-year love affair between Octavio and the cello. As he grew, the cellos grew, too, from quarter-size to half-size to full-size—friends that matured with him. Each instrument had different wood, a different personality. You had to get to know each one like you would get to know a person. There were times when you needed to touch it with infinite gentleness and others when you clutched it furiously.

Only when Octavio began to take on the qualities of a man, did he understand how profoundly the cello was like a woman: vocal as a woman, shaped like a woman, and it had a range of feelings as vast as any woman's.

In retrospect (that is, in his prison cell) Octavio realized that when he first met Yolanda it was like rediscovering the cello. Her breath, the warm air that floated out on her voice, her wide hips that he rested his hands on. No wonder she had inspired him to compose so many songs. It was true that under her influence his compositions had become more political. But the ones he always liked best were the simple love songs, and when he played gigs he always slipped one or two into every set. Yolanda shrugged off the songs. "I don't want to be immortalized," she always said, "I just want you never to stop loving me."

Falling in love (1)

Octavio met Yolanda at the *Facultad de Filosofía y Letras* of the University of Buenos Aires in May of 1974. It was a rainy day and cars were honking in the streets. He asked if he could sit down at her table. The café was just across from the *facultad*. Octavio had noticed Yolanda before. He was drawn to her dark eyes and hair, and fascinated by her round face that shined like a moon in shadow. Octavio was thin, like his father, and he liked the fact that Yolanda was softer, fleshier.

It turned out Yolanda's mother was from Mexico and you could hear a bit of her mother's accent in Yolanda's speech. Octavio talked about music that day, talked too much about music, he decided later. Yolanda didn't seem to mind, however, since she agreed to go to a movie with him that weekend.

That was their beginning. Less than two months later they were ducking on a daily basis into a little hotel where you could rent rooms by the hour. There was no other place to make love. Yolanda had a way of taking Octavio into her arms that suggested she was and would always be a buffer between him and the world. Nothing was hard about her: not her voice, not her muscles, not her thoughts. It turned out Yolanda was a virgin (she had told Octavio so, but he didn't believe it at first because so many women claimed that. When he saw the blood on the sheet he felt stupid, sad that he had hurt her). Within a few weeks Yolanda had gotten so she could forget the dirty walls and stained sheets, and slowly their lovemaking became a kind of mooring for their relationship. Octavio always felt he was melting into Yolanda— disappearing into her skin the way you disappeared beneath waves.

Guitar

When Octavio was fifteen he rebelled against his music studies. He had dreams of being like the Beatles and he insisted on trading in the cello for a guitar: a classical guitar, because that was the only kind Tudor would consider buying with the money.

After that Octavio sat upstairs in his room picking out melodies on the instrument. Graceful little turns decorated the air. His fingers danced among the strings, zipping up and down in arpeggios. He got better on the instrument, and pretty soon Octavio was playing for other people: at school, at bar mitzvahs, later at the university.

"I know who you are," Yolanda told Octavio that first day in the café after they finished their third espresso. "You're the one who plays here in the evening sometimes."

So she had heard him! Every Friday night the owner of the café pushed the tables back from one end and had live music. Octavio sometimes played there with two Chileans. Folk music, mainly: Dylan with *charango*.

At first Tudor didn't want to come hear Octavio, but when he finally relented, he gave it his blessing.

"Good, though not as good as Bach," he told Octavio. "Just remember: play music but study law!"

Octavio didn't bother to tell his father what they both knew by then: that Octavio was never going to study law. He was hardly even attending classes anymore. Afternoons he went to the hotel with Yolanda. And evenings he played gigs at different bars around the University.

Yolanda (1)

Yolanda was the political one at first. She came from a conservative Catholic family—Italian on her father's side, Mexican on her mother's side. Her father always said that the only good Communist was a dead Communist. Peronists, he sometimes chuckled, should just be maimed.

Everyone knew the Philosophy Faculty was thick with leftists. "*¿En qué andás?*" her father asked her one day. "Are you a member of the Communist Party yet?"

When Yolanda said she had become a Peronist, her father was so relieved she didn't say she was a communist that he forgot to get angry.

Her father's reaction was different when he found out she was sleeping with Octavio, however. He had gotten suspicious about her late-night studying and asked a friend to tail her. The friend saw her going into the hotel with Octavio.

"*¡Puta de mierda!*" he shouted at her the second she came through the door that night, "You goddamn whore!" He had been drinking and started thrashing her on the spot.

Yolanda tried to break free of him, but couldn't. Her mother was standing in the doorway to the bedroom, crying and wringing her hands.

"Why are you just standing there?" Yolanda screamed at her. "Why don't you do something?"

Because her father was so drunk, Yolanda managed to twist free and get out the front door. She wandered for hours before she finally showed up at Octavio's house a little after sunrise. No one was up yet but Octavio's mother.

"*¡Pobrecita! ¿Que te pasó?*" Renate exclaimed when she opened the door.

Yolanda spilled out her story in sobs.

Then Octavio's mother marched Yolanda upstairs and put her to bed in the guest room.

Yolanda's stopover

Yolanda stayed with Octavio's family for two days until her father calmed down. Finally, Tudor was sent to make everything right with Yolanda's parents. He set off with a bottle of French liqueur and a box of chocolates.

"And tell them the Seder story," his wife told him as he left that evening. "Tell them about the nun. They're Catholic, they'll like it."

Which is what Tudor did.

"On the train from Rumania a nun took care of me," he

told Yolanda's parents. "You might say the Catholic church saved me."

At first they listened skeptically to his story about his mother and the train ride to Holland.

"The nun got on just after we crossed the German border. Her name was Katrina—*Sister* Katrina—and she was going to Maastricht. When she realized I was Rumanian and a Jew she told me to stay by her side. It took a day and a half to cross Germany. She gave me food to eat. In Berlin Station she changed trains with me. Before she got off in Maastricht, she made the conductor promise to keep watch over me until I got to Amsterdam."

Yolanda's parents heard him out.

"Since that day I have always gotten along well with Catholics. If my son and your daughter have fallen in love, I credit the nun who saved my life. Perhaps our children were fated to join our two religions."

Anyway, the visit worked, and by the time the night was up, Tudor and Yolanda's parents had drunk the liqueur, eaten the chocolates, and agreed that Yolanda should come back home.

"Also, you aren't to go to the hotel anymore," Tudor told his son when he got back.

"But *Papi*," Octavio pleaded, "there's no place else to go."

Tudor thought for a moment.

"At least don't go back to the same one," he shrugged.

Falling in love (2)

After their first few months together, Octavio knew he was truly in love with Yolanda, in love in a way he had never experienced before. It occurred to him that he had discovered in her a whole new world that he would never be able to explore in its entirety, even if he dedicated himself to nothing else. He composed love songs for her and sang them to her late at night. One day when he lay smoking a cigarette in a hotel they frequented (a different one, yes), he said to her that he wanted them to start making love in a bedroom of their own.

Yolanda was brushing her hair and watching him in the mirror.

"What are you talking about?" she asked.

"It's simple," Octavio told her. "I'm asking you to marry me."

Yolanda took a deep breath.

"But you're Jewish," she said. "What will your family say?" What she really meant was, what would *her* family say?

"I've thought of that," Octavio said matter-of-factly. "We can have a civil ceremony."

Still, at the wedding they smashed a glass with their heels anyway (jointly, however, as Yolanda had recently discovered Women's Liberation). Then they danced all night. Tudor bought them a little bungalow on the outskirts of Buenos Aires as a wedding present, and they went straight there for their honeymoon. That first night, Octavio told Yolanda he was the happiest man in the world.

Yolanda told him she thought she was pregnant.

"That makes me happier than the happiest man in the world," Octavio replied solemnly, and they both collapsed in laughter.

The detention center (2)

The men were kept upstairs on the main floor, the women down in the furnace room. The interrogation room was down there, too—it must have been a fruit cellar originally. Octavio often tried to picture what the chalet had looked like before it had been converted. Who had built it? And why?

And how had it passed into the hands of the military?

He imagined a family coming out to the chalet in December or January. During the late forties or early fifties. They would have taken the train, since it wasn't likely they had a car back then. Then a taxi from the station.

How many children? Two? Three? As best Octavio could reconstruct the original layout they must have had three or four small bedrooms. Nothing fancy. The two upstairs rooms had been divided into little cells (Octavio's was the smallest). The other cluster of cells was probably originally the kitchen. Funny, the bathroom had been left untouched. When the guards took you for a pee, you could almost convince yourself that you had stepped for a moment out of the detention center and into someone's vacation cottage. It seemed almost as though you should be able to turn around afterwards and go out to lie in the sun or take a swim.

But no.

Still, in his mind Octavio pictured a little boy and girl running around outdoors, scrapping with each other, playing in the woods, riding bicycles over the bumpy roads.

He always tried to picture the chalet as it had been in the past. But when he could not keep the present at bay, he would return in his mind to Yolanda, wondering whether she was somewhere down in the basement. Was she being held there, too? Or had she perhaps never been in the same detention center?

And what was happening with their baby? In his mind Octavio tried to track her pregnancy: five months, six months, seven months. It occurred to him one day he might already be a father without knowing it.

The worst thing was never knowing. Not knowing isolated you completely. There was a guard who seemed a little nicer than the others, but the one time Octavio tried to get some information out of him, the guard told him to shut up or he would be taken down to the interrogation room.

Politics

Yes, Yolanda was the political one: well intentioned, naive, hoping for a better world, hoping to help her fellow man. It was so innocent, really. And so hard to believe she could be a threat to anybody.

There were meetings. Octavio and Yolanda had a house and it was convenient to meet there sometimes, though they were careful not to draw suspicion. At least that was what they thought.

There was also Octavio's music. In 1975 he started to mix his love songs with more political material. Sometimes it was not the songs in and of themselves, but the little comments he ad-libbed. In fact, sometimes it was not even *his* comments. People in the audience took advantage of the anonymity to call out things. "*¡Viva Allende!*" was a common one.

There were always some undercover policemen in the crowd. One night the security forces raided Octavio's concert. They checked everyone's identification papers and took away two fellows. One of the policemen took a long, hard look at Octavio's identity card.

"*Pibe, ¿estás buscando problemas o qué?*" he asked with what seemed like genuine concern. "Why are you looking for trouble?"

Then he sent Octavio home.

After that, Octavio kept more to his love songs in public. But he and Yolanda compensated by hosting more secret meetings.

The abduction

Octavio knew perfectly well what hit him that day in 1976 when he was kidnapped, even though it all happened so fast. He had come close to being grabbed once before in his friend Guillermo's house, so he knew the tune.

He was on his way home, with about a block to go. His slow-motion realization that men were descending on him and the blow that knocked the wind out of him seemed to take place at one and the same time. Before Octavio could do anything they had blindfolded him and thrown him into the back of a car. Someone pushed him down on the floor and covered him with a blanket. One of the men kicked him periodically.

Octavio felt the car speed away from the neighborhood where he had lived as a married man for less than a year. For some reason he found himself wondering what it would be like to watch the trees receding from that angle. He thought of Yolanda and panicked at the realization that they had probably already been by the house. Then he pictured his mother and father and knew they would cry when they figured out what had happened.

"This is where the real fun begins, *pibe*," one of the men in the front seat shouted back to Octavio. "You won't get much sleep tonight." That was all they said to him for the whole trip.

Octavio wanted to cry but couldn't. Most of all he was cold. The floor of the car was freezing.

The fear seized him that they were taking him to the Naval Mechanics School. But he turned out to be wrong. From the lack of traffic noises Octavio knew they must be headed away from the city. When the car stopped and they pulled him out, it was to march him up to the front door of a quaint little chalet.

("I hold myself responsible for everything that has happened," Tudor told his wife one night in late 1976. The old man had found out a month before that he had cancer. "I just want to die," he said.

"Tudor, shut up!" his wife snapped. Why did men go weak at the strangest times? They could be so strong at others! She kept a picture of Octavio and Yolanda on her nightstand now.

"I should have sent him away," Tudor continued. "I can no longer live with myself."

"It's not your fault," Renate said softly. "Mothers are supposed to see these things coming. *Your* mother did!" She sighed. "But we thought everything changed after the Second World War. How could we know this would happen?")

Guillermo's (1)

That afternoon in *barrio Flores* should have convinced them to tone things down—the day Octavio and Yolanda and another couple nearly got kidnapped. They were at Guillermo's apartment, waiting for him to get home. Octavio knew where Guillermo kept the key, and they let themselves in.

The four of them were having coffee when armed men smashed the door down with a single blow.

"Freeze, or we shoot!" one of the men shouted.

They had come for Guillermo. In seconds, ten men entered the little apartment.

"What the—?" Octavio's friend started to ask, but he got a rifle butt in his stomach before he finished his question.

"Where's Guillermo?" one of the men asked Yolanda.

But Yolanda couldn't manage to get a word out. She just shook her head.

"Listen, you subversive little bitch, don't hide anything or we'll take you, too."

But Yolanda just stood there shaking her head.

It was Octavio who finally had the presence of mind to speak. "We're not subversives." He tried to stay calm. "We can't be on any list."

The leader of the squad stared at Octavio, not sure whether to be outraged or amazed. Still, something held him in check—perhaps nothing more than the fact that a team of human-rights workers from Holland was visiting the capital. Things like that sometimes made the paramilitaries a little cautious for a few days.

"Who gives the orders here?" he finally demanded.

"Just that we won't be on your superior's list if you call," Octavio said quietly.

"*Basta!*" the man shouted and stomped out of the room.

But from the bedroom they could hear him dialing, then giving their names to someone at the other end. There was a long silence. Finally they heard the man's voice again.

"*Bueno, está bien*." You could picture him nodding. "Right. Okay."

The man reappeared in the living room. Without saying a word, he shoved their identity documents into Octavio's chest.

"Just get the hell out of here," he said.

Guillermo's (2)

When Octavio told his parents what had happened at Guillermo's, Tudor pronounced it a good sign.

"You have had your brush with fate," he said. And referring back to the story he always told at the Seder, he added, "This was your Berlin Station. This was your Passover."

Octavio's mother's eyes filled with tears of joy.

"You're safe! And you have confirmation that they aren't after you!"

"This is like a baby falling off the bed before six months," Tudor added. "It protects against something worse happening."

Then Octavio's father offered a prayer of thanks.

"This is Providence," he added in closing, and that seemed to say it all.

The baby

When Yolanda went into labor, her cellmate Alicia started banging on the walls. After what seemed like forever, a guard came.

"She's having a baby!" Alicia shouted when the guard opened the door.

The guard looked at her. "What do you want me to do about it?" he shrugged. "Do I look like a doctor?"

But there was a woman in the other cell who had worked as a midwife. They dragged Yolanda in there.

It was a long labor, over twenty-four hours. In between cramps, Yolanda thought of Octavio. She prayed for it to be a boy, prayed over and over for God to give her a son—a strong, healthy one who might stand a chance of surviving. She had known two other women who had had babies in jail, and they had both died.

"It's better than the military stealing them," another prisoner said one day. It was common knowledge that the guards gave—or sold—babies to barren military couples.

"But I want my baby!" Yolanda had answered. And she wanted it now. She wanted it so desperately that, hour after hour, when her stomach seized up on her, she pushed, pushed with all her might. She felt like a train was roaring through her, like she was turning her guts inside out, like fire was spreading through her bowels. And when, the next day, the midwife, calmly taking Yolanda's pulse during a particularly severe cramp, suddenly exclaimed, "It's starting to crown! I can see the head," Yolanda felt a ray of hope.

Now she really bore down. The baby was an enormous weight that she was trying to push uphill through her body. The women around her encouraged her and wiped her brow, but Yolanda knew that it was all up to her now. She had to put the baby into the world, she had to do it by force of her guts alone. She pushed and she pushed, and slowly she felt the slow weight move.

"It's coming!" the midwife told her, "don't let up!"

And Yolanda didn't. The little baby was crushing her, but she pushed anyway.

The next thing she knew the head was free.

"Keep pushing!" the midwife cried as she made sure the umbilical cord was clear.

Yolanda bore down again. The shoulders were next, then the buttocks. Finally the thin little legs that looked strangely fishlike slid out.

In the cell the women broke into applause. The midwife had the baby in her hands and now, as Yolanda fell back in exhaustion, she put the child on Yolanda's breast.

As the baby began to nurse, Yolanda heard the midwife's

voice: "A boy! A beautiful baby boy!"

When Yolanda woke again, the placenta was already out (it had practically delivered itself), and the midwife had cut and tied the umbilical cord. The baby was there beside her, sleeping. She thought he was the most beautiful baby she had ever seen.

The next few days were a period of true joy for Yolanda. Sometimes she could hardly believe she was so happy. In prison! How could anyone be so happy in a secret detention center?

The women in the cell all helped her with the baby: washing it when it wet itself, rocking it, suggesting names.

After three days, Yolanda was sent back to her own cell. In the interim she had almost forgotten Alicia, but their reunion was one of laughter and tears of joy. Alicia became like a second mother to the baby. This went on for three weeks.

Then one day the guards opened the door.

"Both of you, on your feet," they told the two women. "Here, put on these clothes."

Yolanda and her cellmate looked at each other. Yolanda stooped down to pick up the baby who was fast asleep on a makeshift mattress on the floor.

"You won't need that," the guard said.

For a second Yolanda didn't know what to do. But Alicia made a sign not to resist.

The guards filed them out and marched them to the stairway. Yolanda could hear the sounds of other prisoners.

"We have a surprise for you," one of the guards chuckled. It sounded sinister, but then he added, "We're showing a film."

But when they returned to their cell two hours later, the baby was gone. Completely gone.

Yolanda started screaming, and she screamed so much that one of the guards came and punched her into silence.

"It stopped breathing, you stupid bitch!" he panted. "During the film. We found it dead."

"That's a lie!" Alicia whispered after the door closed. She was wiping blood off Yolanda's face. "They stole the baby. They stole it!"

Yolanda (2)

In retrospect, Octavio thought that it was only after he and Yolanda were married that he really got to know her. Innocent, idealistic Yolanda. Still half-Catholic, still hoping for a better world.

Yolanda believed things could be changed. Mankind could be saved. In her mind the selflessness of Jesus joined the egalitarianism of Marx.

"Two men with long hair," Octavio used to tease her. "Jewish subversives, both of them."

"In Church they always taught us that Jesus was the first Christian," she countered.

Anyway, Yolanda still believed, in her own way. She brought out her little skeleton figurines for All Souls day, and she liked to visit a cemetery, whether she knew anyone there or not.

It went back to having a Mexican mother who had taken her regularly to churches and cemeteries. Yolanda had always felt that in the dark, cool interiors of the churches the answers to her questions were hidden. Somewhere in the shadows. It was just that her eyes could not quite make them out. She couldn't adjust fast enough from the bright light of outside.

"Yolanda," her confessor used to admonish her, "you think of the world too much."

But it was not that. It was just that her eyes were weak in the dark. There were so many half-hidden corners in the churches. Sometimes as a girl she would go stand in one of them and wait for revelations to come, the way they had come to the saints she adored. But it never happened.

When Yolanda discovered Liberation Theology, it was the

closest thing she had found to a revelation. Octavio would come home and find her reading fervently. The books piled up around her.

Over dinner she would lecture him—earnestly and lovingly—about this new way of viewing God. God was not to be some mythical figure, nor was He disposed to forget human suffering. All that nonsense about only the next world counting was crap! God (if there really was a God, she cautioned) cared about what was happening in the here and now, and people therefore needed to dedicate themselves to relieving the injustices of this world. The Argentinian Catholics were reactionary and out of step with the times, that's why all they did was preach about the next life. In Nicaragua and Guatemala and Brazil the priests had already figured out that preparing souls for the afterlife was not enough!

Yolanda's face shone when she got impassioned, and this was a subject that impassioned her. Octavio loved her that much more for her passion.

Later in the evening, when they went to bed, Octavio would gently caress her belly and whisper, "Let's not forget about the little life in here, either," and he would tap her abdomen where their baby was quietly forming. For, as it turned out, Yolanda had been wrong about being pregnant at the time of their marriage; but a year later something clutched in her stomach one day after they made love. She knew immediately what it was. There was no mistaking this time: she felt as though a little hook had lodged inside her, nestled into the folds of her womb. Yolanda was so sure that she crossed herself the second she realized it.

As if in confirmation, less then a month later Yolanda began feeling nauseous in the morning, and that decided matters.

First interrogation

When they took him into the interrogation room the night he was abducted, Octavio had no idea what they might ask him. He had no idea what he even knew that could be useful. To his surprise they didn't ask him a thing. They shocked him with the *picana*, and occasionally threw water on him to increase the shocks. But they didn't bother with any questions. Octavio had the strange feeling they were just goofing around.

"The revolutionary poet!" the guard named El Macho called him. "The singing Jew!"

Three or four people chuckled in the little room.

After a while El Macho said:"Let's take a little break. Octavio is probably tired. I know I am."

That brought laughs. Someone commented that fighting subversives was hard work.

Octavio heard boots cross the floor to him.

"Is that true, Octavio?" this new man asked. "Are you tired?"

"Yes," Octavio whispered.

The man's fist hit his face.

"You mean, 'Yes, sir!'" he said. "You always say 'sir' here, *entendés?*

"Yes, sir," Octavio repeated.

"Let's let him rest then," the man said jovially.

Then someone was lifting Octavio gently off the metal bed and guiding him down a hall. It was hard for Octavio to walk, and the guard, realizing this, slowed down for him. At one point the man patted Octavio's shoulder, as though to say he knew what Octavio was going through. They turned right. The man touched Octavio's arm again: lightly, to stop him.

From another part of the house they could hear highpitched screams. The two of them stood there for maybe half a minute as the screams floated around them.

Finally the guard leaned over and whispered into Octavio's ear: "If I'm not mistaken, that's Yolanda." He said it casually, almost conversationally. Then as he pushed Octavio forward he added, "*Pobrecito*, don't you see we already know everything?"

The train

The train had lumbered slowly into Berlin.

Tudor watched intently as the farms gave way to houses, then the houses to buildings. The neighborhoods slid by slowly: grey (it was raining) and bustling, all trams and pubs and apartment buildings.

He had heard so much about this city, about what was happening in Germany. Now here he was in its midst.

The film (1)

One day, in January 1977, Octavio got an answer to his prayers. For better or worse, he found out about Yolanda.

The guards came around that day and tossed clothing into the cells, even though it was the middle of a heat wave.

"Get dressed," they ordered.

It was the first time in months Octavio had worn clothes.

Then they gathered together all the prisoners in what had once been the living room. No one knew why, but they had set up chairs in little rows.

They took off the prisoners' blindfolds. Behind them, against the wall, someone had set up a projector.

"You're going to watch a film," one of the guards said. No explanation why. Nothing. It had never happened before. And it never happened again. In the detention center things just took place: logical and illogical things became equated. That way even good events took on a strange tinge, because they reminded you how suddenly it could all change. They could do whatever they wanted with you, and you had no power.

As soon as they pulled off Octavio's blindfold, he saw her sitting across the room, three rows up.

Yolanda! She saw him at the same moment. She was making an effort not to be caught looking back at him. But she knew. He knew she knew because she was waving at him with her little finger from under the seat of her chair.

The film (2)

The first thing Octavio noticed about Yolanda the day of the film was how thin she was. And seeing her so thin, he knew immediately that she had had the baby. Miscarried? At term? She had hardly been showing when they were kidnapped, but she was thinner now.

What had happened to the baby? Had it been premature? Had they taken it?

Yolanda and Octavio were careful not to be seen communicating. The lights went out and the powerful beam of light threw the images of the film onto the screen. Octavio was dimly aware of a well-known Argentine actor, of some kind of comedy: colorful images of a world he no longer knew. Every now and then one of the detainees would laugh at something in the story.

Octavio and Yolanda had nothing more to communicate with than little tilts of their heads and small gestures of their fingers. Still, they managed to get across the basics: "Are you all right?" "I miss you." "I love you."

When the film ended, the guards led the prisoners back to their cells, beginning with the women. As they took Yolanda out, she glanced back at Octavio one last time. The sockets of her eyes were deeper than he remembered. He had the impression she was fighting back tears.

"*Te amo*," she mouthed.

Octavio took a chance. "The baby?" he mouthed back.

Yolanda took an even bigger risk. She brought her thumb and index finger together into a little circle in an A-okay sign, but just as she did so one of the guards pushed her forward. For better or worse, Octavio never saw the gesture.

That night the guards came around and collected the clothing. One fellow in the converted kitchen got caught trying to hide some undershorts, and they took him down to the interrogation room.

In Yolanda's cell, Alicia dabbed at her friend's wounds and tried to comfort her.

After the film

After the film, Octavio returned to his cell, relieved and disturbed. He knew where Yolanda was. And he knew that she was alive.

He also knew that it had probably been true when the guard had told him the screams were hers. When he thought of what they must have done to her, his chest nearly exploded. He imagined she had probably miscarried. At least he hoped so. Octavio told himself that he would rather have lost a baby than to have made one for *them*.

El Bajito (1)

When they came to Octavio's cell one day in early March it was just like when they took you down to the interrogation room. Just the same, and he thought that that must be where they were going. El Bajito and another guy called El Tigre rapped on the door.

"On your feet, Rabbi, you're coming with us." The guards had recently taken to calling Octavio "Rabbi."

Then the door was open and they were hauling him out, each one taking an arm. Octavio didn't make trouble; he had been there too long for that.

Octavio tried to steel himself for an interrogation. He tried to imagine what they might want. Maybe they had arrested a friend of his? He hoped he wouldn't be brought face to face with anyone he knew. Sometimes they shocked you to get you to squeal on a friend. Sometimes they shocked the friend. It was pretty much the same thing.

"Where're we going, sir?" he managed to ask.

"Shut it," El Tigre whispered, and he did.

He tried to think straight, listen to the sounds. Strange, he thought he heard other prisoners moving around, too. Were they all being taken somewhere? Sometimes they moved prisoners around if human-rights workers were coming. Also when they rounded them up to execute them.

They went down the long hall. If they were headed to the little room, they would soon be turning left.

The air was moving around him—that is, people were moving. They turned right and into a little room near the back door of the house.

"Sit down, here," El Tigre said.

They sat him down. Then El Bajito freed Octavio's hands and started to pull off his blindfold. "Here, put these on," El Bajito said and tossed a shirt and pants Octavio's way.

Octavio began to panic then. He tried to say something, but couldn't. When they took you to the back door and pulled off your blindfold it meant they were transferring you to either your freedom or your death.

"It's okay," El Tigre mumbled near his ear, "*quedate quieto.*"

At first the bright light almost blinded him, so that he was not sure if he saw what he thought he saw. He quickly pulled on the clothes.

Then he realized he was right. El Bajito was standing in front of him with a guitar. Behind Octavio were other prisoners.

"Take this," El Bajito said, thrusting the guitar in his lap. "It's the captain's birthday, and you all are going to surprise him with a song. Start singing 'Happy Birthday' as soon as he comes through that door."

Then El Bajito bent down so that his lips were near Octavio's ear. Octavio expected some kind of threat. But to his surprise El Bajito said something completely different.

"One thing," he whispered. "Did you know they leave the front door unlocked every night?"

Then El Bajito stood up and walked away. Octavio forced

himself not to look up. He told himself he hadn't heard correctly. It was impossible. El Bajito couldn't have said what Octavio thought he said.

El Bajito (2)

Or could he?

All that day Octavio thought about this. He had two questions. The first was whether it was true. The second was why El Bajito would have told him, even if it was.

As soon as he could, Octavio whispered the news to Pablo in the next cell. At night they often whispered through the connected drain pipes of their sinks. Octavio wanted to know what Pablo thought.

Could it be true?

And if it was, why would El Bajito tell them?

Pablo said that it was impossible to answer either question. "You either believe it or you don't," he whispered. "It's like the existence of God."

Pablo talked it over with another cellmate and together a small group of detainees tried to recollect whether there had been little, hidden signs that El Bajito was not happy with things. Was there some hint he disagreed with the authorities?

No, they had to admit. Not really. El Bajito had never been particularly bad toward the prisoners, it was true. But he had never done any favors either.

"None of this means anything," Pablo said through the drainpipe. "Maybe he hasn't wanted to give a sign. Maybe he's been waiting the whole time for a chance to help us."

"Or to trap us," Octavio answered.

The discussions went on for a week: furtive, hushed exchanges when the guards were occupied; words whispered into the drain.

In the end, they decided there was no telling why El Bajito had spoken. It could be an invitation to be shot while trying to escape.

118

Or it could their one chance for freedom.

Berlin station

"It turned out Sister Katrina was Dutch, not German," Tudor always paused to mention when he told his story at Seder, as though that somehow explained the event in the station. "But since she was from Maastricht, she spoke German fluently. I thought she was beautiful. I even wondered once or twice if she really was a nun." He would chuckle. "If she had been dressed differently we could have been husband and wife."

Sister Katrina insisted Tudor stay right beside her when they changed trains in Berlin. "She knew no one would bother a nun," Tudor explained. "And she was right. She had me carry her bags."

The train creaked to a halt. Already people were jumping down to the platform. Others were waiting on the quai to meet relatives. Tudor shrank back from plunging into the crowd, but Sister Katrina gave him a little push.

Once they were on the platform, Sister Katrina took the lead. She walked fast: first to the main hall to check on their connection, then they exited from the main hall toward where the westbound trains were located. The quais stretched out from them like long-fingered hands.

"This was a week after *Kristalnacht*," Tudor would always point out. "A Rumanian Jew in the heart of Berlin? Not a good situation. Thank God I had a guardian angel."

Thank God, indeed. For no sooner had they come out onto their quai to wait for the train than Tudor happened to look across the other quais. He only watched for a few seconds, but what he saw was to remain imprinted in his memory forever.

"I couldn't believe it," Tudor explained. "They were about four or five quais away, in a large group all swarming around."

"Who?" listeners hearing the story for the first time would always ask.

But Tudor told his tale the way he wanted to.

"I thought I was dreaming. I only looked over for a moment. Still, there was no mistaking it." Then he explained, slowly and deliberately, "It was the Führer with all of his top brass. There he was, not more than thirty meters away! Adolph Hitler!"

"Are you sure it was the Führer?" people would ask.

"Of course I'm sure," Tudor answered. "Who could mistake that face? Besides, they were all there with him: Goering, Himmler. I recognized them in a second."

"What were they doing?"

The question always irritated Tudor.

"How should I know what they were doing? They were waiting for a train, I suppose. Führers had to wait for trains, too, sometimes." Then he would go on. "But can you imagine what it was like for me to look Hitler in the face one week after *Kristalnacht*? Can you?"

As a boy this question always reduced Octavio to silence. He wondered what he would have done. Would he have turned away? Would he have taken off running? Would he have been able just to keep moving forward—to walk in and out of danger like passing through a shadow? The man who was to have Tudor's whole family murdered—Tudor actually saw him!

"I will never forget the experience," Tudor would say sadly. "I stared at him, and for a second I had the impression that he was staring at me, too. It was as though the Führer was looking right through me. To this day I'm sure he saw that I was a Jew and that I was a terrified. If it hadn't been for Sister Katrina, they probably would have come over and arrested me."

"Why, what did Sister Katrina do?"

"Nothing grand," Tudor would say. "She tugged at my sleeve a little. She had seen them, too." Tudor would always chuckle here. "Sometimes the greatest actions are the most simple. Sister Katrina tugged at my sleeve and made me look away.

Then we climbed up onto the train." In a hushed voice he would add, "During the whole ride to Maastricht we never said a word about what had happened."

Conversation in the sink

"It's worth the risk," Pablo whispered through the pipes one night. "I've talked to some others."

He was talking about trying to make a break for it. Octavio didn't answer right off. He had only one cellmate—Flaquito— and Flaquito was in favor of running for it.

"Are you with us or not?" Pablo asked.

"When?" Octavio whispered back.

"The night of the third. The new moon." There was a calendar up in the living room and one of Pablo's cellmates had managed to study it for a few seconds. "We'll be harder to spot if they come after us. What do you say?"

"I have to think about it," Octavio said. The third was in four days.

"We can't waste this opportunity." Pablo's disembodied voice gurgled up through the drain. It was as though he were already far away.

"Just let me think," Octavio repeated.

Tudor (2)

Toward the end of 1976, when Tudor knew he was going to die of cancer without seeing his son again, he wrote down a long message—half-letter, half-testimonial—for Octavio, should Octavio ever show up.

Their rabbi was against it.

"You must be realistic about these things," the rabbi said. "You must accept the present. The past is the past." He said it more for Octavio's mother than for his father. The rabbi was worried about how she would fare on her own, always hoping for the impossible.

But she couldn't accept what the rabbi said either.

"The truth is not always pretty," the rabbi added. "Our people have always suffered."

Meanwhile, Octavio's mother hoped against hope. Sometimes when she had cried too much, she blamed Yolanda's politics for getting them into such a mess.

"Octavio always made his own decisions," Tudor would answer.

There were also better days when something in her heart told her her son's was still beating, too.

In his letter to his son, Tudor told the story of Berlin Station one last time. "Remember this tale, my son," he wrote, "and learn from it." He also expressed his concerns for Octavio's mother. "If you live to read this," he wrote, "you have an obligation to do all you can for your mother, for she has suffered much, maybe as much as you have."

The cancer crept into Tudor's liver a couple weeks after Hanukkah in 1976. On New Year's eve he was in a lot of pain and had to be taken to the hospital. The doctor explained that there was little they could do from then on. "Painkillers to keep him comfortable," he said, "that's about all."

Then began the slow process of Tudor's withdrawal from the world. He got thinner and thinner, and the things he said made less and less sense. By February he no longer recognized his wife. The end was near and they gave him morphine injections on a regular basis.

When Tudor died he was buried in a plot he had bought in the forties for himself and his future wife.

They held a small ceremony. Yolanda's parents came and left rocks at his grave.

Tudor (3)

After the funeral service for Tudor, Yolanda's mother went with Octavio's mother to her house. They went upstairs and sat in Octavio's room and wept together in silence. For the first time, Renate had real doubts.

She tried to feel her heart beating—tried to feel the sympathetic rhythm of her son's own heart somewhere. It was terrible to think that Octavio was out there somewhere, suffering, and that she could not locate him. A mother's love should be able to locate anything, she told herself. How many times in the streets of Buenos Aires had she told herself that for all she knew she was passing right by where he was? If only she could see what was behind the facades of the buildings!

It was even more terrible to think that Octavio was gone forever. Yet, for the first time she thought that was maybe the case.

"Tudor is dead," she suddenly blurted out in a rush of tears, "they have taken our children from us!"

Yolanda's mother put her arms around Octavio's mother.

"We must keep hoping," she said softly. "We must always keep hoping."

She was not sure whether Renate was listening or not.

But how could you have hope? As Octavio's mother raised her head and looked around the room, she saw all the little trinkets and trophies Octavio had collected during his childhood. She felt a deep rage within her that it all should have been taken away like that. She even felt anger at Tudor. It was as though he, too, had deserted her, leaving her alone to face the death of their son.

Tudor, with his faith in Providence and his stupid belief that things would work out in the end! She could not partake of such optimism. It all rang hollow to her, and into that vacuum rushed doubt.

Octavio's mother doubted everything now. Maybe they had killed Octavio and Yolanda the very night they kidnapped them. Maybe she had been hoping in vain all these months.

Perhaps not even Tudor had had any hope. Maybe he had only pretended, pretended all his life. He had always told that story about Berlin Station but, now that she thought about it, she had to admit that he hadn't really talked about his family very much. Only that they had all perished.

Instead he had clutched to his miraculous tale, repeating it every year like an article of faith. It was his talisman.

Renate looked around the room: at the pennant for the local soccer league, at the secondary school diploma, at a little photo-machine picture of Yolanda taken shortly after Octavio met her. The bookcase was filled with the books Octavio had read—whole volumes of words that had poured into his consciousness. Where was that consciousness now?

And what did she have except her memories?

Perhaps what Tudor had understood was that what was remembered was everything. Only what got remembered— what got passed down from generation to generation—was real. Tudor's whole family had perished, and Tudor alone had been saved. Over and over he told that story of being saved. Perhaps he needed to believe it. Perhaps he wanted to believe.

It suddenly occurred to Octavio's mother that perhaps Tudor's tale of Berlin Station was not true after all. Perhaps it had never taken place—not the Dutch nun, not Adolph Hitler standing a few quais away from Tudor. Nothing.

What, she asked herself, if Tudor's story had just been made up to give the rest of them hope? What if the miracle of Berlin Station had been nothing more than Tudor's private myth?

Octavio

Octavio did not know what to do. For him it did not come down to El Bajito and his message—whether or not it was true, whether or not the escape was a set up. For Octavio it came down to Yolanda.

Could he leave Yolanda? Was it better for him to stay or to run?

"What's your answer?" Pablo whispered through the pipe on Thursday night.

"*Todavía no sé*," Octavio said. "I still don't know."

There were so many questions. Could he even be sure she was still downstairs? He had seen her back in January, but that was no guarantee she was still there.

"What would you want her to do?" the voice in the sink whispered up to him.

The question stumped Octavio. There was a long silence. Finally he bent down and put his lips to the drain.

"I would want her to leave me behind," he said slowly. Then he added, "At least, I hope that's what I'd want."

On Friday things were still no clearer.

In his mind Octavio kept imagining both possible scenarios. He watched them over and over in his head as though they were films. First he saw the cell door quietly open and then he and the other men were all tiptoeing to the door. The living room revolved around him as he got to the front door. Then he ran the other film in his mind, and he saw them leaving, only now he stayed seated in his cell. The line of men slowly moved away from him, like a memory vanishing. Octavio tried to imagine what they would find on the other side of the front door, and he tried to conceive of what the guards would say if they found him alone in his cell, come morning.

"I might not know until the moment comes," he finally confessed to Pablo. "What more can I tell you?"

Waiting

The second hardest thing on Saturday night was the waiting. Pablo insisted that they wait until they knew the guards were downstairs for the duration. That meant waiting until the early hours of the morning. Then the plan was for them to pull their blindfolds partly off, cross the floor as quietly as possible and file out the front door one by one. They had managed to shimmy the cell doors on Friday and knew they could open them at a moment's notice. Pablo and his men were ready to go. So was Flaquito.

"They'll kill you on the spot if you stay," Pablo whispered through the pipe. "You know that."

"You're probably right," Octavio answered.

But could he live with himself if he left Yolanda behind?

That night she was all he thought about. He recalled the days and nights they had spent together. He thought of the countless times he had held Yolanda in his arms, and of the way they had looked at each other after the close call in Guillermo's apartment.

After that afternoon, they had sworn eternal fidelity—a different fidelity from the marital kind. A deeper one.

"We swore never to abandon each other," he whispered to Pablo.

"I swore allegiance to the Communist Party," Pablo replied wryly. "What does that matter now?"

"This is different," Octavio said.

"Besides," Pablo finally said a little harshly, "for all you know she's been transferred."

Finally there was a tap on the wall.

"We move in five minutes," Pablo whispered through the pipe.

The second hardest part was almost over.

The men all knew that the hardest part was going to be opening the front door and stepping out. Not physically the hardest, but psychologically.

They had an agreement that if they got to the front door and it was locked, they were to get back into their cells as quickly but also as quietly as possible, with no panicking. If they were lucky, the guards would never know anything had happened.

Each man tried to picture opening the door and stepping out. Octavio had a feeling that if the men were not hit immediately with a hail of gunfire, they stood a real chance of escaping.

He told Pablo so through the pipe.

All Pablo replied was, "One minute."

Yolanda (3)

The anonymous phone call to Yolanda's parents one night in late April didn't say much.

A man's voice: "If you want your daughter's body, I'll tell you where to find it. Take down the following directions and go there tonight."

The caller described a field on the edge of town. He knew what he was talking about. Yolanda's father took a friend with him. They found her in a shallow grave. The stench when they opened the ground almost knocked them over. There were other graves, you could tell.

They were lucky and got a doctor to take a look, but he couldn't tell them much. "Pretty decomposed," the doctor said. "Could be a couple weeks. Could be a month or more." He found the bullethole at the base of her neck. "At least she died quickly," he told them.

The family convinced their parish priest to give Yolanda a Catholic burial. While Father Muraldo intoned hymns over the grave, Yolanda's mother looked around her. She wondered about the voice that had called. A good samaritan? A sadist? She studied the group of mourners. Could the caller be among them?

The wedding night

For some reason Octavio was thinking about his wedding night. He remembered how they had made love that night in their new house. It had not been the best lovemaking of their lives. Weddings never were, because people ate and drank too much. Still, he had felt a sense of infinite abandon that night with Yolanda, as though nothing were so large or powerful that it could ever pull them apart. He had sensed the bond literally, physically.

Octavio even remembered lying in their new bed afterwards, naked, and staring at the thick liquids that clogged the hair where they had made love. He had joked that it was the glue that bonded them.

Octavio thought of his parents. He wondered if they had felt the same union. He wished he had asked his father, but it would have been impossible. He suspected that *he* might have been the glue between his father and mother. He alone.

The end

This was the longest minute of their lives. But when it finally took place, it seemed the most natural of actions. Magically, dreamily natural.

Suddenly there Pablo was, opening Octavio's cell door from the outside. Flaquito was already on his feet. It seemed impossible that it was happening, but it was.

Octavio had not even heard Pablo's men open any cell doors, they had been so silent. And now here was his own door thrown open! The men were already filing out of the cells on either side of his. Pablo looked once at Octavio and nodded. With one hand Pablo held Flaquito back while the others filed by. The men were too scared to look at each other.

Then Pablo waved Flaquito into the line. The first man was almost across the room. Pablo crossed the floor now and took the door handle before the man reached it. This was the moment of truth.

With a flip of his wrist, Pablo turned the handle and pulled. The door opened to reveal the darkness of night. Octavio could see the stars, and even from his cell on the other side of the room he could feel the fresh breeze.

He thought of Yolanda as he saw Pablo step across the threshold without so much as a pause. The men began to file out the door behind Pablo. With powerful force Octavio had a revelation that the escape was going to be a success. And he had an intimation—a vision almost—of Yolanda standing in the night air, there beyond the threshold. Her arms were stretched out to him, and she was calling him from some distant place that was no longer of this world. It was as though he could see her, floating there in the night sky, and singing now as well.

In a final rush of thought Octavio realized that this was it. This was the final moment. He knew he was losing Yolanda, had lost her, that he would never see her again in this world. There was only one place to find her now, and that was in the night—a night as vast as the one that spread forth from the front door.

In spite of himself, he uttered her name aloud.

Siobhan Dowd of International PEN's Writers-in-Prison Committee in London writes this column regularly, alerting readers to the plight of writers around the world who deserve our awareness and our writing action.

Silenced Voices: Zouhair Yahyaoui
by Siobhan Dowd

*O*nce there were *samizdat*, photocopies or hand-printed bulletins passed around by hand, in a bid to circumvent the proverbial blue pencils of censorship. Today there is "cyberdissent." Dissidents launch websites with secret access codes, and proxy addresses for when the authorities try to intervene; the audience is anyone, the world over, who

Zouhair Yahyaoui

has a computer and a telephone line. Unfortunately, the exciting means of censorship busting offered by the new technologies do not seem to afford any more protection than dissidents had of old. Even if cyberdissidents use pen names for their online activities, the governments whom they attack have their own means of tracking them down.

So the Tunisian editor Zouhair Yahyaoui has found to his cost. AKA "Ettounsi" ("The Tunisian"), Yahyaoui, the founder of a popular and flourishing webzine, was arrested last June and is now serving a two-year prison term. His "crime" appears to be in part his sense of humor: his lively magazine invited readers to vote on whether Tunisia was a "republic, a kingdom, a zoo, or a prison." The results of this interesting poll are unclear, however, because not long after it appeared, Yahyaoui was seized by members of Tunisia's security services at his place of work (a cyber café on the outskirts of Tunis). He was escorted back to his house, which was then searched without a warrant, and taken into custody. For forty-eight hours nobody was told of his whereabouts. But visitors to his website found that its pages were no more.

Yahyaoui, thirty-four, is a graduate in economic sciences living in Tunis. He is engaged to his colleague, Sophie Elwarda, and has a loyal circle of friends. One associate describes him as an autodidact and a nature lover, who, even when he is bursting with a million ideas, never forgets to water his plants. "He has chosen his own way in life and does not hide himself away. He talks big, both at home and in public. He talks loudly sometimes, and allows himself to say what others only think... He is a national treasure, and a force for international understanding."

True to his type, Yahyaoui found his own brand of employment when he graduated, with his discovery of the endless possibilities of the Internet. He founded www.TuneZine.com, which rapidly became the most popular virtual space in Tunisia. The site ran scathing reports of human-rights violations in the country, critiques of the fifteen-year-long regime of President Zine al-Abidine Ben Ali, challenges to the tourism industry, and discussion boards for visitors. What started as a one-man band expanded to a nucleus of five people, mainly talking to each other by email. His fiancée, Sophie Elwarda, who has reinstated the website as a campaign springboard for his release, comments that the reason for the clampdown was the magazine's growing influence. "It was starting to have a real impact. It was being consulted by all Tunisia's opposition elements. We were often being quoted… Although it was already being censored, we had found a way to divert the censorship by connecting ourselves to another server."

The most recent issue of TuneZine contained, in addition to the humorous poll, several articles analyzing a constitutional referendum held on May 26, 2002. The official tally claimed that 99.52 percent of voters approved the President's bid to run for a fourth term in 2004, and granted him immunity for prosecution. TuneZine questioned the validity of the poll and claimed it had been anti-democratic in the way it had been run.

Another factor that seems to have led to Yahyaoui's arrest is the fact that his uncle, Judge Moktar Yahyaoui, became internationally prominent after he wrote a scathing open letter to the President denouncing the lack of judicial independence in the country, stating that Tunisian judges "render verdicts dictated to them by political authorities, and enjoy no discretion to exercise any objectivity or critical scrutiny." The letter became a *cause célèbre*; Uncle Moktar Yahyaoui was fired, reinstated, harassed, followed, and denied permission to leave the country. In a possibly related case, his daughter was assaulted by a stranger with a truncheon. When Zouhair was arrested, his uncle immediately issued a statement in his defense, noting the TuneZine had been one of the first places to publish his famous open letter, and that the magazine was simply a much-read forum for debate, with no criminal tendencies.

After his arrest, Yahyaoui was pressured—some report that he was tortured—into revealing his website's access code. He was charged with "propagation of false news" and "non-authorized use of an Internet connection," and sentenced to twenty-eight months' imprisonment, later reduced to twenty-four months. Yahyaoui declined to attend his hearing, saying he did not "trust a justice [system] that followed orders [from above]."

Sophie Elwarda reports that she is extremely worried about the conditions of her fiancé's captivity. "More than eighty men share a single room. Sometimes there isn't even enough space to sleep," she claims. "They only have water for half an hour every day." She reports that his family members are permitted only one visit a week, and that any nutritious food they bring is confiscated. An unconfirmed report in September suggested that he had indeed been mistreated, and that he had also suffered from a kidney complaint which caused him to be briefly hospitalized. He is now said to be in a prison some twenty-eight kilometers from Tunis, and concern for him mounts.

Yahyaoui went on a two-week hunger strike in January to protest his continuing imprisonment, but to date he has not been released, despite the many international appeals on his behalf.

Please write polite letters appealing for the immediate release of Zouhair Yahyaoui to:

His Excellency Président M. Zine El Abidine Ben Ali
Président de la République
Palais Présidentiel
Tunis
Tunisia
Fax: 011 216 1 744 721

Mika Tanner

My father built this swing for me. I loved it.

Mika Tanner has an MA in Asian American Studies from UCLA and is currently earning her MFA at the Iowa Writers' Workshop. "Lists" is her first short story accepted for publication.

MIKA TANNER
Lists

My wife is stopping by the house today so I'm trying to tidy up, make things presentable. Ever since she moved out two months ago, the place has been a bit of a mess. Nothing out of hand or anything—I am quite neat, really—but everything is a little dusty, things scattered here and there in uncertain piles. I go over the carpets efficiently with a vacuum, then wash a plate and mug from this morning's breakfast and put them in the rack to dry. I am sorting through yesterday's mail when the doorbell rings. I check myself in front of the mirror and then open the door.

"Hi," I say. Yumi looks at me, not smiling. She's sizing me up, I can tell. Trying to see how much I've deteriorated since the last time she saw me. I haven't, though, not at all. I look the same as I always have, much younger than my thirty-nine years.

"Hi, Minoru," she says, coming in. "How are things?"

"Great, great," I say cheerfully, setting out a pair of house slippers for her to wear. "Can I get you something to drink?" Yumi shakes her head no. She sets her small white purse on top of the dining table and looks around the living room without saying anything.

"Well," she finally says. "Should we get down to it then?" She sits down and pulls a small yellow notepad from out of her purse.

"All right, sure," I say, and pull up a seat next to her. I can smell her perfume; I don't recognize it. Her old scent was Chanel No. 19. I used to buy it for her on her birthday. The new perfume is much bolder, sweet and sticky like gardenias. I don't care for it. It makes her smell like a different person, somehow, someone I don't know.

Yumi is all business. At the top left of the page in her notepad she writes "Minoru." To the right she puts down "Yumi." Then she makes a straight line down the center of the page.

"So," she says softly, "where do we start?"

I had expected this, but it still manages to surprise me. I examine the yellow pad of paper. What she's written looks like a score sheet for the card games we used to play together when we were first married. Yumi was never very good; I used to beat her all the time at gin.

"Well, Minoru," she says. "How do we do this? Do you want to tell me how you think things should be divided or should we go over everything in each room together? What do you want to do?" She looks at me, two faint vertical lines between her eyebrows. I think about it for a second, but suddenly, the thought of the two of us going over every little thing in the house and assigning it a legal beneficiary seems rude and grotesquely morbid to me, like we are dispensing the worldly effects of a relative who isn't even dead yet. "You go ahead and do it," I finally tell her, trying to feign disinterest in the whole matter. "You divide things how you want and I'll just look it over when you're finished."

Yumi squints broodingly at me, thinking it over. "All right," she agrees. "I'll do the first pass." Then she says sharply, "But I don't want you interrupting and getting all upset if you don't like something I've written down. Please, let's try and discuss this civilly, okay?"

"Of course," I say, somewhat offended. "How else would we do it?"

Yumi goes straight to work. I go into the kitchen and pour

myself a cup of coffee. I stand there with it and stare out the window above the sink. Two small boys from the house across the street are playing some kind of game in the driveway, running around and around in circles. As I watch, the smaller of the two trips and falls flat on his face. His brother is bent over laughing as the younger one lifts his head up with a look of dumb amazement. Then he screws up his eyes and pinches up his mouth all tight as though he is about to start crying. But his brother stops laughing, goes over to him, and lifts him up off the ground. Next thing you know, they're running around in circles again like nothing happened. Kids, I think. So foolish.

I go back into the living room and sit down at the table once more. I glance at the progress Yumi has made and then watch her bent over the notepad, making her lists. She's biting her bottom lip in concentration. She's wearing a blouse I've never seen before, a bright green one with buttons down the front. It's quite nice. I have to admit, actually, that she is looking good, better than I've seen her in a long time. My wife has long, densely black and evenly straight hair that she keeps off her neck in a clip; no dye jobs or shag cuts for her, hairstyles that even the women in Japan all seem to want to wear. Fortunately, although we have been in this country now for five years, Yumi is still quite old fashioned in that sense. And her eyes, well, I've always thought they were really very pretty. They're almost as black as her hair, and elongated like a cat's. They give her face a very languid, sultry look, especially in contrast to her hands. She has tiny hands that are always moving, swooping around her face. She makes them flutter like little birds when she talks; it's very graceful. When we first met I used to watch her hands the whole time she was saying something to me. Sometimes she'd have to repeat what she had just said because I had been so caught up staring at them.

Suddenly I'm swept over with a strange feeling of homesickness for her. My love, I think, the words sounding unfamiliar even inside my own head. My wife. I had promised myself that I wouldn't do this, start wallowing in the syrup-heavy comfort of daydreams, and yet, my resolve at dignity is beginning to crumble. How can this be happening, I wonder. My life is changing so fast these days that I'm having trouble recognizing it. One day I am quite contentedly married and living a life that no one could really complain very much about, and then I wake up and my wife is gone and the sky has fallen down around me. It's like being on a plane that's about to crash: you know you're doomed but you're praying you'll survive it anyway. You keep thinking there might be a chance.

"Hey, Yumi," I say softly. "*Neh*—"

She stops working on her list and looks at me. "What?" she says.

I want to say, Are you sure about this? I want to tell her we can work it out, that we'll take a trip somewhere, just the two of us, do our best to save the life we've built together. Act like Americans and hope that by doing something romantic and sentimental everything will be okay. But I don't say anything. I have known, as soon as Yumi expressed her desire to leave me, that sweet words could never fix something so desperately in need of repair. The way I see it, if something is that irreparably damaged, it is better for all concerned to leave it that way, rather than try and cover it with band-aid-thin promises and hopes. I owe the two of us at least that much, I think.

"Oh, never mind," I tell her, and then continue to look at what she's writing. I notice that she's taking all the china and glassware that we've collected over the years. Let her have them, I think. I don't need it. Like most men, I have never been one to get excited by plates, no matter how pretty they are. She's the one who wanted to buy all of it in the first place, talking on and on about Wedgewood and Royal Doulton, comparing china patterns and all that. I couldn't even tell you what the stuff we own looks like, but even so, something claws in my chest despite myself, some part of me that makes me turn away from Yumi and look down at my hands. I clasp them in front of me for a second and then examine my fingernails. They are clean and have just been cut; seeing them makes me feel better.

When I look up again my wife is looking at her hands, too. She has them spread out in front of her and she's watching them as if to make sure they are hers. I observe that she's taken her wedding ring off. I've taken mine off, as well. In this time of crisis I have tried to stick to my practical nature, to let things happen the way the universe has willed it. To do anything else would be simple foolishness, a feeble knocking on a door that is shut forever. Despite my noble intentions however, I can't quite bring myself to throw the ring away, so I've put it in a box along with all the other relics of my past, letters and photos and such. But I must admit it's quite a shock to see that Yumi isn't wearing her ring anymore, either. I wonder what she has done with it; maybe she has thrown it away, flung it into the ocean back to Japan.

Suddenly, she looks me in the eyes. She is wearing a grimly patient expression on her face that I'm not used to seeing. "Minoru," she says. "I know you're having a hard time with this. I know it. But do you know what I think? I think all this will be good for you, too. I'm hoping that it will force you to take a long, hard look at things, maybe make some changes in your own life."

This irritates me. Who does she think she is, talking that way? She was obviously trying to sound "liberated" and "independent," qualities they seem to stress so much here in women. "What changes?" I ask. "I'm not the one who's unhappy with things; you are. I have no complaints about my life. I'm a good husband; I've done everything that can be expected of me. You're the one who thinks that's not enough."

Yumi's eyes narrow into slits. "You're right," she snaps. "It's not."

This is ridiculous, I think to myself. She would never act this way in Japan. It is being here that has done this to her, made her into just another stupid American woman. In this country, women have no sense of decency—they whine and complain about men and their fear of commitment, want to have their wedding and their white dress, but as soon as they've got the poor fellow where they want him, as soon as they've made him into a solid, dependable rock they lean on for almost ten years, they change their minds. Suddenly they find his company stifling, they need a change. Suddenly they're moving out and making lists, dreaming of men they can never have or, if they could have them, would slowly change into the men they had just so easily disposed of. These women think this is being courageous and strong, that is what is so outrageous. I look over at Yumi and wonder who it is she's dreaming of, if there is someone else already. Is that why she looks so good? Because she's already in love?

Yumi has refocused her attention on her lists. She's taking the sofa, the dining table, the bookcase, and the wicker armchair we bought when we first moved to the United States five years ago. She's giving me the coffee table, the easy chair, and the 32-inch television we bought last year at Best Buy. I, of course, also get to keep the piano and my large collection of jazz records and CDs. I have recordings of all the greats: Duke Ellington, Charlie Parker, John Coltrane, Charles Mingus, Bud Powell. The most sublime music in the world, in my opinion.

To tell the truth, it was my love for American jazz that made me fairly excited when the international shipping company I work for decided to transfer me indefinitely to Los Angeles. Ever since college, when I first became acquainted with this magnificent musical form, America has always held a special allure for me. I had always thought what a wonderful thing it would be to live in a country where such music is created, where men's spirits can find such magical expression. I pictured myself in dim, smoky bars, listening to the soft wail of the trumpet, the sinuous melodies of the saxophone. But even more importantly, I imagined myself having the time to learn how to play the piano, an instrument I have always loved. I dreamed of being able to train my own fingers to play that beautiful, soulful music. Unfortunately, besides the fact that I have had trouble finding any dim, smoky bars in Palos Verdes, the pristine suburb the company moved us into, I am required to spend a large amount of my time at the office. Because I work for a Japanese company, albeit one located in America, I'm still expected to do business the Japanese way, putting in long hours at the office and frequently entertaining clients out on the town or on the golf course. Life here has provided no relief from these exhausting professional obligations, and so, of course, the piano that I rented upon first coming here sits quietly untouched in the living room, used as a place to display photos and the various knick-knacks that Yumi and I have accumulated over the years.

I'm sure that for Yumi, things were a little bit harder than they were for me. After all, my life didn't seem to change too much. At first, she was so impressed by the grandeur of the new house—so roomy compared to our cramped apartment back home!—as well as the newness of everything here, that she had no time to be unhappy. But then, with me at work all day, and her not being able to drive, and having no real friends to speak of, she didn't have anything much to do but try and make sense of all the American programs on the television and clean our already immaculate home. So after a couple years of this, Yumi decided that she was ready to get pregnant and start a family. I, of course, thought this was a wonderful idea. Then, at least, she would have something in common with the other Japanese women in the neighborhood, something to ground her in domestic normalcy rather than the loneliness I knew she often felt. And besides, our parents in Japan had been anxiously waiting for her to get pregnant for quite some time. Unfortunately, things didn't work out the way we had hoped. When we finally went to the doctor, it turned out Yumi couldn't have kids, that she was sterile. This, of course, was terribly devastating to her. "I'm a failure," she would say to me, her eyes spilling over with tears. "I'm a failure as a wife and as a woman." I told her it wasn't her fault, obviously it just wasn't meant to be. To be truthful, I was quite disappointed myself; I had become increasingly excited at the thought of having a son or daughter to raise. I had thought that maybe the piano would finally get some much-needed use.

After a while, Yumi started becoming very serious about the idea of adopting a child. She wanted to go and get a little baby from China or Korea, or India—one of those poverty-stricken places where there are unlimited supplies of babies needing to be adopted. She wanted to rescue it, she said, wanted to give it a chance in life. "For goodness sakes, Yumi," I would say to her, "we're not talking about a dog from the pound, here. This is a serious matter, what you're suggesting. Have you really thought about it?"

"Of course," she'd snap. "Do you think I'd mention something like this on a whim?" Then, softer, more wistfully, "Please, Minoru, please think about it. The child would still be ours—it would still be our baby. Perhaps we would even love it more, you know, because it really needed us." Her eyes would get very round and pleading, like prayers.

Of course, I considered it, but in the end, I had to put my foot down. I just wasn't really all that comfortable with the idea of adopting a total stranger. It seemed like such an unnecessary risk. In my opinion, there is a lot to be said for family history, for genetics and DNA. What if the child's parents were crazy people or criminals, or just plain idiots? You would never know—there would just be no way of knowing that kind of thing. And then you'd be tied forever to this person who might be retarded or grow up to be a lunatic, or possibly worse. It just didn't sound like a good idea. Yumi was quite distraught for a while; we used to fight about it constantly. Eventually, though, she came around. I like to think she saw the logic in what I was saying. After all, it made good sense.

After that, she began claiming that staying in the house all day made her depressed. To my amazement, she learned to drive and eventually enrolled as a student at the local community college. She began studying English, taking marketing courses, and I don't know what else. She also became friends with quite a few of the young Americans that she met in class, students who returned to the same school year after year, trying to postpone their adulthood as long as they possibly could. There was always a certain intensity in her eyes when she talked about her new acquaintances, which, I must admit, disturbed me a little. She seemed to consider their aimless pursuit of fulfillment as something profound, something admirable. Why, I wondered, did she seem to envy them so much? Did the thought of floating directionless, like a bubble, on the surface of one's life appeal to her in some way? Did she hope that by virtue of befriending these people she could forget who she was? But I tried to push these feelings out of my mind and be supportive of her endeavors— after all, I am not the sort of husband who demands his wife be home to pamper him and cater to his every need. As long as she did not neglect her main duties around the house I could find no real reason to object to her studies. To be perfectly truthful, I believe that everybody should improve their minds if they have the opportunity and the leisure to do so. In fact, I envied Yumi a little bit—in my opinion, married women these days, married Japanese women in particular, are quite spoiled. They are not tied to a job the way we men are, do not have to spend their lives working, carrying the burden of their family's survival on their shoulders. They are quite able to become a carefree student again, or play golf all day if they want to. If only I were that lucky; I would know how to play the piano by now, maybe even have a weekly job at a nightclub. I'd tour New York, Kansas City, and New Orleans, listen to jazz all night long, smoking Mild Sevens and losing myself in a sweet, bebop-tasting haze. Certainly I wouldn't be here in prim Palos Verdes, the responsible managing director of an international shipping company, dividing all my earthly possessions with my wife on a yellow pad of paper. The shipping company is a very good place to work, don't misunderstand me, but it's tedious. Sometimes it's hard to think that this is the most I can expect from life. But what can I do? It is a respectable job and they treat me well. In Japan, there would be no question that I was a lucky man. But I do not let myself indulge in these kinds of thoughts too often, because if I did, what would become of me? Discontentment is not something I can easily afford to feel.

Yumi gets up from her chair and starts wandering around the living room, examining things. She goes over to the bookcase behind the sofa and brushes the bindings of the books with her fingers, lightly. "I'll take these books, if that's all right with you." She takes a book from its shelf and starts flipping through its pages. I can see the title, written in Japanese, from where I'm sitting. It's called *Mrs. Craddock*. It sounds familiar, but I can't recall if I have ever read it. I used to read quite voraciously when I was younger, but it has been a long time since I have had any free time to sit down with a book. When I am able to find a little time for reading these days, I like to skim the newspaper so that I can know what's going on in the world.

Before becoming a student, Yumi never used to read a great deal. In fact, I used to encourage her to pick up a book on occasion, since I have always thought it important to have at least a rudimentary acquaintance with the great literature that has been produced throughout the centuries. At the time, she didn't seem all that interested, but, in the past couple of years she has begun to read quite ravenously, some books in English, but most of them in Japanese. Every week she'd be reading something new, something she picked up at the library or the Japanese bookstore in Little Tokyo. She'd read in bed, as well, which, to my annoyance, made any romance between us impossible. Once, I remember, she was reading *The Great Gatsby*, which, I'm well aware, is an undisputed classic work of literature. Yumi couldn't stop talking about it, she loved that book so much. She thought it was so incredibly sad and romantic, just beautiful, she said. Of course, I had read the book years before, and I remember that I had liked it, too; besides finding it to be well written, I had thought it was a very interesting portrayal of American society during that particular time in history. But I also remember being quite irritated with it—Jay Gatsby's reckless, swooning adoration of Daisy had always struck me as weak and unmasculine. No matter that Daisy was nothing more than a very silly woman, and that she was married—Gatsby was bent on making a perfect fool of himself over her. And yet, in most readers' eyes, certainly in my wife's eyes, he is the embodiment of romance, the quintessential tragic male hero. I remember sharing my opinions very candidly with Yumi, and that she did not take them very kindly. She didn't talk to me for hours after that.

Yumi puts *Mrs. Craddock* back on the shelf and picks up a blue Chinese vase painted with birds that my supervisor at work had given me back when we had first moved here. She turns it around in her hands, looking at it. Both of us love that vase; we put it right on top of the television so that you could admire it from every angle in the living room. The sight of it unexpectedly smears something in my heart, leaves small, sticky thumbprints all over it. "Yumi," I say casually, trying to disguise the longing in my voice. "Remember how nice Takeshi-san was to give us that vase? I've always thought it looked quite lovely displayed in the living room. Don't you think so?" I am hoping that the sight of some cherished object will spark a look of tenderness in her eyes, but they are expressionless, all dense, black pupil.

"This vase?" she asks me. "I've never cared for it at all, you know that. Remember, I always used to say the birds on it looked like evil crows—they scared me. I only put it up in case we ever had to have Takeshi-san over to the house for some reason. I had no idea you liked it so much. Of course, then, you should have it. That's fine." She writes it down on my side of the list. I look at the vase and she's right, the birds do resemble crows, rather mean and sinister looking. I had never noticed.

What else have we looked at differently, I wonder, from different angles, with different points of view and standards of taste? Have we always been so opposed in our thoughts, deceiving each other with our agreeableness? All this time, has Yumi seen things I have been blind to? But no, if anything, it is the integrity of her vision that has changed. Where I see a perfect expression of beauty, she sees only crows, menacing black figures of doom. That is not sight, in my opinion.

Yumi sits down again at the table. She has finished listing everything in the kitchen and living room and is now moving into the bedroom with the relentlessness of an army tank. She writes "bed" and "bedside tables" on my side of the list. Then she pauses, scrunching her eyebrows together unattractively as she thinks. I know what it is that's made her stop. She's thinking about the dresser. It's this antique walnut piece that we bought together a short time after moving to America. It was our first piece of furniture we bought here, and it is still probably the nicest thing we own. It has four large drawers and two smaller ones on top with very pretty little glass knobs on them. We would never have been able to fit something so huge in our apartment back in Japan, so when we first bought it, it had seemed especially impressive. In a way, though it seems ridiculous now, the dresser had embodied our hopes for our new life here: polished and shiny and enormously grand. Looking at the expression on Yumi's face, I can tell that she wants to take it away with her, keep it for herself.

"What's wrong?" I ask innocently.

"Nothing," she quickly says. Then, "Well, I'm wondering what we should do about that dresser in the bedroom. I was maybe hoping that you'd let me have it. You know how much I love that piece."

"I know, I love it, too. It's a beautiful piece. I'm rather attached to it myself."

Yumi levels her eyes at me. "Well, I guess I'm giving you the bed and the bedside tables, so it seems only fair that I get the dresser. I picked it out, remember?"

"What difference does it make who picked it out?" Suddenly, it feels like it will kill me to see her writing it down on her side of the list. It is quite irrational, but I decide that I really want that dresser, more than I've wanted anything in a long time. I can't imagine living without it, the emptiness it will leave in the bedroom if it is gone

"Come on," she says. "Please, be reasonable. You're getting to keep just about everything else."

I consider it. But there's no going back now. It is a pride thing, almost. I don't want to lose. "Yumi, that dresser is very valuable. I don't need to tell you it would cost a fortune to replace it. And, since you are the one who has decided to leave, it just stands to reason that some things, you are just going to have to give up."

Yumi crosses her arms over her chest and leans back in her chair. "I knew you'd be like this," she says. "I knew you wouldn't make this easy for me. Very well. You take the dresser then. I don't want to argue about it with you anymore. Why do you insist on being so difficult?"

"How am I being difficult?" I demand coldly. "I'm just doing what I can to keep my life in order with the least amount of inconvenience and expense. You have no right to blame me for that, especially since it is you who has caused it to fall apart."

My wife looks down and rubs her forehead, something she does when she is upset. "Yes, Minoru, you're right. It is my fault, all you're going through. I wish it didn't have to be this way."

At her words, something like hope breathes inside of me. For once, I do not suffocate it, but let it sift inside my chest, waving its airy tendrils of faith. I want to look her in the eyes, but she keeps her head down, still rubbing her forehead with her fingers. "Yumi," I say, doing what I told myself I'd never do. "Is that true? Is that true what you just said? Because it doesn't, you know. It doesn't have to be this way. Nothing has to change if we don't want it to." I reach out and touch her hand. She blinks moistly at me for a second, then quickly moves her hand away.

"You told me that you understood and respected my decision," she says firmly, her air of regret quickly vanished. "It's no use trying to talk me out of it now, after all this time has passed. I've got to move on."

"Move on to what?" I snap, upset at myself for making such a naïve, foolish gesture. "You don't have any idea what you're doing. It's ridiculous, a woman your age. People in Japan are going to think you're a fool."

"I'm not going back to Japan. I'm staying here, I thought you knew that. I'm going to remain a student, stay here on a student's visa." Her eyes are gleaming with pride and excitement. But me, I'm absolutely flabbergasted. I had just assumed she would go home. "Yumi," I say sternly, "what do you think you're going to do with yourself, how do you think you're going to live? You have no job, no way to earn money. What are you going to do when your visa runs out? You can only stay a student for so long, you know." I eye her suspiciously and begin to wonder, despite myself, if she has already found a man who is willing to support her. But she shakes her head at me impatiently. "I'm going to find myself a job here. Under the table for a while until someone is willing to sponsor me for a work visa. Don't you see, I'm making changes in my life, finally. I'm changing how I see things, how I think about them, and that allows me to live my life differently, with freedom. I can't do that with you or in Japan. Look, you don't even know what I'm talking about. And really," she says, "this is not what I came to discuss today. I just wanted to start taking care of things here, wrap up some loose ends." She checks her watch and then says, "Maybe we can talk some other time. I have to go now. I'm supposed to be somewhere in twenty minutes."

Yumi takes a look at her lists, four pages of them, my stuff and her stuff all neatly divided. She tears the sheets from the notepad and pushes them in front of me. "So, how does this look? Can you live with this?"

I look over the lists. If it's a score sheet, I'm not sure who's won. So much there, yet I don't know what it means to me anymore. There will be big blank spaces all over the house once she takes her things out. It makes me depressed to think about it. I'll have to go buy a new sofa and dining table right away, although I do not look forward to living with things that will smell unfamiliar, have no past. I cast an eye on the couch, the comfortable, cream-colored bulk of it, trying to picture it in the middle of Yumi's new apartment, which I have never seen. And suddenly I have a vision of her sitting on our couch, the couch we bought when I got my first promotion, the couch that we used to relax on for hours on end, reading peacefully together or watching television. Yes, she's sitting brazenly in the middle of those memories with some faceless man, both of them disheveled and draped across the plush upholstery with the lewd abandon of teenagers, grinning wildly and nuzzling and touching and...

I grab the list, hold it up to Yumi's startled face, and rip the pages straight down the middle. I lay the pieces calmly on the table, the "Minoru" side and the "Yumi" side forever separated, not only by irreconcilable differences, but by a viciously resolute and jagged tear in the sheets of yellow notepaper.

My wife's mouth has dropped open as if on a hinge, the whites of her eyes clearly visible around the dark-brown iris. "What are you doing?" she screeches. She looks at me, surprised more than anything else.

"Just forget it," I tell her, trying to sound cool, but feeling the sweat begin to gather under my arms. "Just forget this list of yours, this will you're making, like everything is so nice and easy and bloodless. Coming in here picking and choosing like you're at a shopping mall."

"Minoru," Yumi says, her voice dangerously quiet. Her glare is murderous. Where did she learn to look at someone that way? "You're being an idiot," she says. "This was my house, too, you know. All I'm doing is trying to salvage my life and be happy. You may see it differently, but I'm not doing this to you—it's just the way life is. I'm trying the best I can to make this as painless as possible, but if you can't handle that, then fine. We'll do it another way." She picks up the scraps of yellow paper and puts them in her purse. She walks to the door and opens it. I follow her. "Goodbye, then," she says, pausing at the threshold. Her eyes stare into mine, liquid brown-black heartbeats, pulsing at me. I don't say anything, just close the door behind her. I listen to the *click-click* of her heels down the walkway, and then hear her get into the car and turn on the ignition. She drives off, the whine of her engine fading as she turns the corner.

I go to the sofa and sit down. I stroke its nubby texture with my hand, owning it with my touch. It's still mine, I think to myself. I turn the television on to the local news. Traffic accidents, a random shooting, insurance rates are going up. A chemical spill on the freeway, embezzlement charges filed against a local CEO. Los Angeles is a terrible, dangerous place. Whatever Yumi may say about seeing things differently, there's not a lot I can change about how I see the state of this city, that's for certain. Maybe I should move back to Japan. Maybe if I went back, it would be easier, things would make more sense. Here, things just happen to you; you can't do anything about it. But, of course, that is ridiculous. Things have changed everywhere—Japan and America, they might as well be the same place. I won't move and I know it. For better or for worse, right now, this is where I have to be. I have my job to think of, after all, as well as my parents in Japan, who are getting on in years. Unlike Yumi, I will not fall for the easy lures of this country and forsake all that I am, all that I have ever been. She believes that it will be easy for her to do this, but I know better. She'll discover the truth soon enough, I suppose.

I continue to watch the news, but Yumi keeps creeping into my thoughts like a cold mist. What is she doing now, I wonder. Is she on her way to meet the man of her dreams for dinner, that faceless, dark-haired man who isn't me? I picture her in her green blouse, her hair swept up and off her face. She's talking to him, right up close to his ear, her laughter like champagne bubbles wafting up toward the surface. The man turns toward her, his eyes full of a love and tenderness that are almost palpable. The man is not faceless. The face is mine; I am that man. I reach down and take Yumi's small, birdlike hand in my own and touch it to my lips. She smiles at me; whole books are in that smile. Yumi, I think. My love, my wife. 🕴

Quinn Dalton

My mother worked hard on my stick-straight and tangle-prone hair, shown here with a soft and entirely artificial wave. A beautiful, smart, and fiercely devoted woman, my mother has always wanted me to feel I looked nice. Thanks, Mom.

Quinn Dalton graduated from the MFA Writing Program in fiction at the University of North Carolina Greensboro. Her first novel, *High Strung*, is forthcoming from Simon & Schuster's Atria Books in July 2003, with a collection of short stories, *Bullet-Proof Girl*, to follow in 2004. Her stories have appeared or are forthcoming in literary magazines such as *Story Quarterly, Mangrove, Cottonwood, Emrys Journal, ACM (Another Chicago Magazine)*, the *Baltimore Review*, and the *Kenyon Review*. She is the winner of the Pearl 2002 Fiction Prize for her short story, "Back on Earth." She lives with her husband and daughter in Greensboro.

QUINN DALTON
Midnight Bowling

*I*t was Mr. Ontero from across the street who found my father stretched out in the front yard next to his IV tree as if he'd gotten tired of waiting for someone to let him in. Lettie and Harold Bell and fat Ms. Parsons and the triplets, and other people whose names I don't remember anymore, stood on the lawn watching Mr. Ontero trying to save him while my mother was at work and Donny Florida and I were at school. It was a cloudy day and still pretty brisk out, typical Ohio spring; I imagine the red and blue flashes splashing the treetops on our street like the disco lights dotting the Star Lanes. Mr. Ontero checked my father's pulse and puffed into his lungs because no one else would do it. In between breaths he told the neighbors he was an old man and had seen the Spanish flu, and everyone had said the world was ending then, which it hadn't, so he wasn't scared of any so-called plagues.

After the funeral Mr. Ontero offered to sell back our lawn mower at the price my father had sold it to him. "Fair is fair," he said to my mother on our doorstep, tulips from his garden quivering in his outstretched hand. "No profit-mongering here."

My mother slammed the door in his face. A couple of weeks later, when I started back to school, I'd see Mr. Ontero as I walked to the bus stop, bent like a question mark in his front

Glimmer Train Stories, Issue 47, Summer 2003
©*2003 Quinn Dalton*

yard, picking leaves and twigs from his silky, trimmed lawn and stuffing them into his pockets. Whenever I stopped to say hello he told me stories about making lard soap in the Depression and earning a dollar a week on the oil rigs in Missouri City; he spoke like a typewriter, in a kind of emergency Morse code, never pausing to allow me to say "that's nice" or "goodbye" until I had to walk away or miss my bus. I'd hear his voice trail off like a plane passing overhead and feel too embarrassed to look back.

Then Donny started giving me rides to school and work whenever his car was working, and I hardly saw Mr. Ontero at all until he died last week. I rode my bike to the funeral in my pink Eatery waitress uniform, having just been fired, to say goodbye to him in his casket.

Now Donny's driving me to orientation, and I'm thinking about Mr. Ontero as a little boy, cutting the tip of his nose off with his toy plane propeller and having to sit still with no anaesthetic while they sewed it back on with thread, real thread; and my father swimming in dark Lake Erie to impress my mother; and Mr. Ontero's squinty black eyes, the last to see my father alive. His reedy thin voice hums in my ears on and off during the two-hour drive, while my mother thinks I'm at work, saving money for our big move. The voice is saying, "You've got moxie," which he said every time I won the Junior Tournament Bowlers Association of Ohio—Rookie of the Year when I was thirteen, Bowler of the Year at fourteen, and Highest Average the next two years. My father put the trophies in the front window to signal each win. He was Joe Wycheski, the Buckeye Champion of the Ohio Bowlers League eight years running. Donny's uncle Leo, who owns the Star Lanes, puts your picture on the Hall of Fame wall if you get the Buckeye three times. My father's picture has a permanent space in a gold-speckled plastic frame.

Donny pulls into the visitor lot, singing at the top of his lungs to Led Zeppelin. A girl pulls in next to us in a red convertible and hops out; Donny doesn't notice her crinkling her nose as if she smells exhaust from Donny's brown T-Bird with the racing stripes he painted himself—she's walking fast, bangles clinking. A gold chain gleams on her ankle.

"I'll meet you here," Donny says, and for a moment I forget why I thought this was such a good idea, going to college, where he won't be.

The first session is Campus Culture. The tour leader, a blonde woman with a pointy chin that turns white at the tip when she talks, says State has a strong gay/lesbian association, and the girl with the bangles says fags shouldn't be allowed because it runs against the Bible, which is why they're being punished with AIDS. Nobody says anything to this. Of course now people are saying you can get AIDS from mosquitoes, or saliva, and that we're all being punished.

Then there's the Student Services and Learn the Library tours, and a packed lunch, and at the end I'm in the parking lot waiting for a half hour with my slick gold and black folder, looking at this wide green campus filled with people I don't know, wondering if there's any good lanes around. I watch the girl with the bangles get in her car and drive away without looking at me, even though she smacked gum in my ear for five hours. Donny strolls from behind some buildings like he's at the park, in no particular hurry. He stomps out a cigarette, unlocks my door first.

"Where were you?" I ask.

He shrugs, doesn't answer. We get on the highway again. "You know what I heard," he says, not asks. "If you can't go to college, go to State."

I roll my window all the way down and hot air blankets us, wisping hair out of Donny's thin, rubber-banded pony-tail. Donny hates driving with the windows down, but I like it, because it feels like flying, like the roller coasters at the park.

"Oh really?" I say. The road melts air at the top of the next hill; radio announcer's drilling the record temperature and humidity. At night, planes crisscross our town, spraying the mosquitoes breeding over ponds. I turn the air conditioning on, to compromise.

"They don't care about you," Donny says.

"You just don't want me to go."

"Whatever." Donny shoves another tape in the deck, Rush this time, singing, *Exit the warrior / Today's Tom Sawyer*. Head swinging forward on the guitar and drums.

What I know is, Donny applied to State, too; didn't even type out the forms. Sent it out like it was no big deal. And didn't get accepted. We haven't talked about what he plans to do this fall, unless he goes full time at the lanes like his Uncle Leo wants. Me, I just got fired from waiting tables at the Eatery because I forgot to bring ketchup to some guy. A bottle of ketchup. I didn't know what I was going to do until Mr. Todd told me about his wife's brother who works at the College of Arts and Sciences at the university, which is weird to think about, a college inside a university. He said his wife's brother would nominate me for a scholarship, even though I've already missed all the deadlines. He called yesterday and told me to go to orientation, said he had something for me. He said there's no need to talk about it to anyone, because these scholarships are for special cases. But I did tell Donny, because I want him to know everything.

"I'm taking a nap, okay?" I say.

No response. I lean back and close my eyes, AC mixed with hot outside air rolling over me in waves, music vibrating my ribs. Donny's driving because my mother finally sold my father's car, which I was using, because she says we need money for our future more than we need things. Our future, according to my mother, is at the Savior Missionary in Marietta. The Savior, as she refers to it, is where I can get real-life experience. "Millions are waiting for the Lord's word right here in Ohio," my mother informed me yesterday. For two thousand dollars, I can get into the missionary program and travel all over the country handing out fliers and visiting foster homes. She thinks I'm going to save that much from waiting tables. So I've been going to work with Donny; I wear my Eatery uniform and change in the bathroom at the lanes. Leo's paying me under the table to balance the books, says he can't see the numbers anymore.

My mother often can't see details that don't fit her "vision," or "God's plan for us," such as the fact that I've slept with Donny, which she decided not to conclude upon discovering a package of condoms in my dresser drawer while looking for my boat-neck sailor top. Or that she's wearing her seventeen-year-old daughter's clothes and dyeing her hair a lot. Or that she's exchanging love letters with a forty-year-old married man named Jake.

Yesterday I wanted to tell her there was no way I was going to Marietta, but then she said we could sell the house and get away from here together and start a new life, and her eyes were shining and her face was flushed, and I couldn't bring myself to do it. Because I want to get away, too.

My mother went to the Savior a couple of months ago for a conference, *Faith in the Eighties,* and met Jake, who actually just lives across town, except now he is a reformed Episcopalian and went to the Savior to rescue his soul. He's apparently perfect for her, except he's married, so my mother and he write each other letters and talk about Jesus' will. They actually mail them to each other, like the apostles, they say. I know because I've read them, locked in the bathroom pretending to take a shower, which is what I do when I need privacy. My mother believes in privacy, meaning not being naked in front of anyone unless you're married, or unless you're an innocent child, which neither of us is anymore.

I steal Jake's letters from Time-Life books stacked along the wall underneath the couch. They are stacked there because she gave away our coffee table, along with most of our furniture and all of my father's things. My mother gives things away because the Bible says to. "We won't need any of this where we're going," she said the day the church van came to pick up our kitchen table and chairs. That was two weeks ago. Now we eat our meals standing at the kitchen counter.

I guess my mother thinks I don't look at those books anymore, at the 1920's discoveries of Egyptian tombs and artists' renditions of the solar system. But I found the letters right away, because I still like to imagine the dry desert heat, the pyramid shadows sliding over sand, ancient priests worshipping glowing planets. I've only seen one of my mother's letters, since she mails them while I'm pretending to be at work. The one I found in a stack of bills and long-distance Bible study offers wasn't what I expected. While Jake talks philosophy, she talked plans—what do houses cost in Marietta? she wanted to know.

After I read the letters, I take off my clothes and stand on the toilet with the water running, inspecting myself in the mirror until it's too steamy to see. I don't know what I'm looking for. Sometimes I try to imagine what Donny sees when we're doing it, how I look from above, or bending over him, or from behind, when I can get him to do it that way.

My mother says I am one of the cleanest people she knows. She says it like she knows something is up. She has started threatening to make me pay the water bill. After I read the letters I put them back between the exact pages of the exact books where I found them.

Donny rolls up the automatic windows, and I turn my head and sigh, still pretending to be asleep, and for a second it feels like we're in space, every sound wrapped in silence, and then I really do fall asleep. Then we're slowing down, sunlight sliding orange on my eyelids. Donny puts the car in park and I hear the seat squeak as he leans across to kiss me. I want to turn away, because I am annoyed with him for reasons I can't explain. But I know it will hurt him, especially after he took me all the way to State and back, so I let him think he's waking me with a kiss. Snow White. I watch him through the blur of my eyelashes. He always closes his eyes, which also annoys me. I open my eyes and stick my tongue all the way into his mouth, and then I start laughing. He pulls back, surprised, then comes at me, head down, trying to lick my face. He slides his hand up my T-shirt and pinches a nipple. I sit up and grab his hands and then I see my mother's car in the driveway, a surprise. Also there's Jake's minivan with the matching car seats in back. I thought they were volunteering at the Terrace Spirit senior citizens' picnic all day.

"I gotta go in," I say, grabbing his hand. He manages to lick my nose and lets me go. I wipe my face with my T-shirt, leave my orientation folder on the seat.

These days our house smells of bleach. My mother carries a spray bottle of cleanser around and washes her hands whenever she thinks of it, which is often. I find her in the living room, flipping through the *Greater Marietta City Guide*. Jake's on the deck, drinking a can of pop and smoking. He keeps cases of pop in the minivan, now that he's sober. He wears khakis and knit golf shirts with athletic shoes all the time. He doesn't know I'm here or he'd be coming in to give me one of his tight hugs and ask me what I've been praying for.

Deliverance, I'd like to tell him.

On the walls are plastic-framed religious paintings, the kind you can buy mail order in three easy payments. They don't quite cover the pale rectangles where my father's pastels used to hang—a historical study of duck and candle pins, lightning over a lake, a pregnant woman in a sheer nightgown standing at a window—all given away. The woman was my mother, but her face is turned away, so no one would know. But my mother didn't think it was "appropriate" anymore. She has told me she won't give away any of my stuff because that's up to me: I have to find my own place in God's plan. Still, I worry. There are things I don't want to lose, like my AMF Angle bowling ball and my father's shirts, which are

Buckeye beige with "Wycheski" sewn in maroon cursive on the sleeve and shirt pocket.

I lean over her shoulder, moving slow so as not to catch Jake's attention, which isn't easy since a lot of things I do seem to get his attention, like when I sunbathe or wear mini skirts, but he drags on the cigarette, squints into the back yard, oblivious. My mother's hair is pink in the sunlight; she doesn't look up. She's wearing one of my halter tops and my favorite Chino shorts. Now, when I find her looking through my closet, she explains it's because she's given away too much and has nothing to wear. She studies a page in the *Greater Marietta City Guide*, glossed lips pursed, penciled eyebrows a frowned line. There is a photograph of gleaming white Victorian houses on the river. Advertisements for complexes like Eagle's Crest and Indian Falls. There's sparkling pools and work-out rooms, happy blond families strolling from their concrete patios to their minivans. My mother drives an old Buick. The spy car, as my father used to call it. Neither of us is blond, at least not right now.

"Aren't these places built on Indian burial grounds or something?" I ask her, and immediately regret it. Jake hears me; he bear slaps the sliding glass door open and lumbers in, grinning at me, neck muscles straining the collar of his Polo. "Tess! The Lord be with you!"

"Hi, Jake."

Jake moves in for the hug. He's blunt and square, an ex-football player, impossible to get around. I think of squeezing behind the couch but I know this is not an option, so I just hold my breath and let him wrap one meaty arm around my shoulders and the other around my waist so my hips jam forward and my nose presses into the hairy V of his collarbone. Behind me, I hear my mother snap another page. She misses a lot.

"How's business?" I ask when he lets me go. Jake sells disaster insurance, which is odd since he believes the world is ending, and how do you insure for that? In the meantime, he talks about God like He's some cosmic weatherman or the neighborhood fortune teller, always ready with free advice.

"Glorious!" Jake says, smiling as if he might break into song. "Your mother and I were thinking you should have your own policy."

I look at my mother and she looks at me, smiling distractedly. I sit down next to her, angling for a better view of the *Greater Marietta City Guide.* "I'm not kidding about the Indians, Mom. Isn't it bad luck to build on consecrated ground?" I point out. Also, the river gave people malaria. I learned this in Mr. Todd's American History class. I also took journalism with him, which was my college-prep elective last year, and he says I could be a good reporter because I call it like I see it.

"There's no such thing as luck," my mother says, ruffling her fingers, mixing my words into the air. "How was the Eatery?" she wants to know, glancing at the absence of my uniform and then turning back to the Dogwood Estates.

I bend to inspect the mosquito bites on my ankles. "The bugs are terrible," I say, scratching. My mother makes a face and stands up. She brings back a bottle of peroxide and a paper towel from the kitchen.

"Listen, honey," Jake says, landing next to me. The cushions sag in his direction, pulling me to him like the black holes in the Time-Life books. I concentrate on not crossing my arms. "About the insurance."

"What, are you going to knock me off, Jake?" I smile at him and touch my upper lip with the tip of my tongue, enjoying how his eyes focus on it. He is gathering himself for a response; I can see a thought working up his brain stem, but my mother beats him to it.

"Where were you all day?" she asks, pushing the paper towels and peroxide into my hands. The latest letter from Jake advises her not to get angry at me if I'm FLIPPANT, to act NONCHALANT because it stumps REBELLIOUS TEENAGERS. Jake writes in all block letters, underlining for effect. Mr. Todd says never to underline. He says it's a sign of immaturity.

"I was with Donny, Mom," I say. I dab peroxide on my bites, which my mom heard on the evening news will kill the AIDS virus in the event it is carried by mosquitoes. I watch it fizz on my reddened skin and wonder if my mother has slept with Jake.

My mother looks out the window, where everything is still and washed out, like an overexposed photograph. "I'm talking to a realtor tomorrow," she says, folding her arms and turning to me, pink-polished nails pressing half circles into her skin. She seems to be bracing herself. Jake watches her bend to hunt though her pile of church bulletins. She hands me a shiny white folder with a red and purple seal and *Savior Missionary* scripted in gold.

"Here you go," she says, smiling as if she just gave me a prize. From the corner of my eye I can see Jake nodding at her. He's obviously coached her on the delivery. I take it from her and open it. Inside are several complicated looking forms including an injury release and a Pledge Sheet with a long list of things I will agree to do and not do, such as renouncing homosexuality, or using the word "Zen." There is a signature line next to a pair of floating hands pressed together in prayer. The application is titled "Foreign Missions Adventure Form."

"This is a chance for you to do something truly great," my mother says, echoing a sentence in the brochure I have just opened. My eyes fall on the words as she says them.

"Praise God," Jake says.

My mother sits on her heels on the floor in front of us, and both of them watch me read. The AC comes on and she shivers. "God has plans for us, Tessie, I really believe that. But we have to win His love. Most people can't do it."

Like your father, she means. I know this because her habit of going to church three times a week and attending conferences and seminars and subscribing to every religious booklist and newsletter she finds only started when my dad got sick a year and a half ago, first with a flu he couldn't shake, then pneumonia, then so many illnesses they couldn't be distinguished from each other anymore. He accused her of trying to make up for him, and trying to make me crazy, but she didn't care what he said at that point. By then you could hardly understand him.

The memory makes my stomach feel tight and bruised. I concentrate on deep breaths, press my fingers into the ultrasuede cushion.

Jake stands up with a grunt. "Tess, why don't you come see me tomorrow at my office," he says, closing in for another hug.

I side step, dropping some papers from the application. "I'm working tomorrow," I say.

Jake picks up the papers and holds them out to me, just far enough away so I have to step forward to take them. He winks when I do. "That's fine. This weekend, then," he says with his song smile. He turns to hug my mother, who doesn't seem to mind his chest hairs going up her nose. "Bless you," he says to her, as if she just sneezed.

"Bless you," she says. She walks Jake to the door, leaving me with the Savior folder and a bottle of peroxide, all the safety there is. There is some soft talking. There is perhaps a kiss. The front door shuts and locks and my mother returns. "I'll need those forms by tomorrow," she says.

"I don't think this missionary idea is the best thing for me."

My mother motions me to the couch. I don't want to, but I sit.

"What is the best thing for you? A waitress job?" She looks at her glossy nails and then at me. "Bowling?" She presses her lips together and waits.

I let this pass. I want to tell her about the scholarship I think I'm going to get, but I decide to wait. I saw the signature line on those forms: parents can sign for kids under eighteen.

My silence seems to satisfy her; she stands, smooths my Chino shorts against her thighs. Perhaps she thinks she's convinced me. Stairs squeak as she heads for her room where, aside from the bed and a few clothes in the closet, she keeps Beta tapes with titles like "Loving God in Pain" and "Self-Denial for Self-Fulfillment." I notice she doesn't count the TV in our required sacrifice.

I hang my feet off the end of the couch. The AC hums; ice drops in the freezer. It's been a year since the overdose, which is how my dad actually died, not from the AIDS. That's how my mom refers to it in private, which she rarely does. As if the overdose was an event all its own, not happening to anyone in particular. Days after they sent him home, my father took all of his painkillers, dragged his IV outside, and collapsed in the front yard, where Mr. Ontero found him while my mother was at work and I was in school. The coroner called it narcotic-induced cardiac arrest. Outside the family, my mother calls it a heart attack.

At the funeral, my Aunt Belinda and Uncle Percy, my mother's sister and brother who live together and take tea bags with them whenever they travel, told me that because my father was a drug addict, I would have to be more careful, I could get addicted to anything. Me standing by the hole with the velvet skirt around it and the coffin looking like it was hovering, about to blast off. Nobody said anything about the AIDS. It was easier to think about the drugs.

My dad's connection was a guy at the molding plant, where they cast the chairs for plane interiors. The police discovered this after the connection left town, and I guess he could be anywhere now, poking holes in people's skin and shooting in just the tiniest amount of his own blood, too.

Weekends my father and I went bowling. He taught me the roll was all in the release. He was wiry, with a little pot belly I made fun of, and thinning reddish brown hair that showed the pale skin and light blue veins of his scalp. He wore button-down flannel shirts tucked into jeans in the winter, button-down cotton shirts tucked into jeans in the summer. After years of making plane chairs, he said he would never fly because of what he knew.

When I was twelve, he gave me the AMF Angle, the first-ever urethane make: custom teal with gold sparkles, teal being my favorite color at the time, with my name in gold. We watched each other in tournaments, holding our breath while the other one glided across the floor. When we rolled for fun, he made me discuss current events and my form, and what I could do to improve it. Mostly, though, he talked about how good I was, and how I could do anything I wanted with an arm like mine.

These days, when I release is when I most feel my father in me, or actually, that I am my father. I feel the ball weight in my shoulder, not the elbow joint, which is where most people tend to hold it, and I know I look like him, and that I'm feeling the things he felt, the light strain at the collar bone, the tightening of the muscles in the back of the arm, the turn of the bones in their sockets as the arm drops, swings back, then forward. I imagine my muscles are his muscles, and this is how I keep him alive.

The last time we rolled was at Rock and Bowl, which is on Fridays from 10:00 P.M. to 2:00 A.M. Donny had just gotten the disco ball and the colored lights—he hadn't talked Leo into the laser and the smoke machine yet. My father had had the flu for weeks by then, but he hadn't been to the doctor. The meetings with teams of doctors and the weeks in the hospital were ahead of us.

His hook was way off that night. "You're pulling the ball," I said. I was annoyed. Once he pulled it five boards or more— amateur mistakes.

He ignored me. "Go," he said, as we watched six pins wobble and stay up.

I rolled and got a strike. When you're on, you hardly feel the weight; it's just a part of you that you let go.

My father powdered his hand. "What's a perfect strike?"

I rolled my eyes. "The ball knocks down the one, three, and five pins," I said. I paused, wondering if he was going to make me recite the whole thing. He was waiting. "The five pin takes out the nine pin, the three pin takes out the six, and the six takes out the ten pin," I said. "The head pin knocks down the two, which knocks down the four, and the four knocks down the seven."

"Close. The five hits the eight pin and the ball hits the nine. You remember that," my father said without looking at me, surveying the lane. He rolled, shuffling forward slowly. Three pins down. Miserable.

I won with the next roll, 168 to 132. Not a good night. "You could've done better," he said.

"So could you," I shot back.

"I'm just saying you shouldn't let your game go. You could get a scholarship, you know?"

I was going to tell him he wasn't my coach and I didn't want to hear his plans for me, but then this happened: he sat down hard in the booth as if someone had knocked his feet out from under him. I stared at him and he gazed back at me, as if this was just a movie he was watching.

He handed me his wallet. "Go pay," he said softly. His fingers were damp and cold.

"Dad?" I said.

He made a sound in his throat and held onto the table. I paid Leo at the bar, forcing myself not to look back at my father, not wanting Leo to see and ask me what was wrong. As I walked back to the booth I felt strangely calm, the sounds of toppling pins muffled and distant.

My father held his arms out to me. "Help me up," he said.

I leaned down to him and he held onto my neck as I pulled him to his feet. Somehow I hadn't noticed before that I was almost his height, and that he was thin, very thin. He smelled sour, like overripe fruit.

"Thanks," he said. I pulled away from him as soon as I felt him balance, and he knew it, and I could sense his eyes on me as I put on my coat. "Let's go to Harry's," he said. He patted my arm, smiling at me, waiting until I looked at him. He was breathing shallow and fast.

"I don't think so," I said. But somehow we ended up there. I remember waving to Donny in the DJ box as we left the lanes—Donny wasn't my boyfriend yet; that would be in the summer, after my father was gone and my mother had let the lawn grow to torment Mr. Ontero—and I remember I could see the sweat on my father's face, but I smiled at Donny anyway and waved to Leo, too, like there was nothing wrong.

I drove to Harry's and my father bought me a beer, which I don't even like, and Harry, who runs a tight ship, didn't say a word about it, even though he knew how old I was. My father drank while I scanned a *People* magazine, at the movie stars and cowboys and sick children starting foundations, and I didn't care for any of it, except for being with him in that place.

Two days later he went to the doctor. Then he went into the hospital—full quarantine. My mother and I had to get tests. A nurse quit rather than take care of him. They couldn't handle him at Carter so they moved him to Cleveland, where at least some of the doctors had seen AIDS before. Then they sent him home to die, and then he killed himself.

So I understand why my mother wants to move. She wants to get away from the house my father grew sick in, from Mr. Ontero's pinched eyes that watched him die in the front yard, from the town that knows our story like it's a TV special.

The voice on the Beta floats through the vents. I'm on my knees, sliding *The Solar System* from under the couch, checking for mail. My heart squeezes tighter, like it does when a roll really counts, and I am measuring the space between me and the strike.

There's a new letter. No postmark—Jake probably hand-delivered this one right before I got home. I slip it into my shorts. "I'm gonna get ready for work," I call upstairs.

No answer as I head down the hallway to the master bedroom, where my father stayed after he came back from the hospital, and where I now sleep. Sometimes I still think I can smell his cologne in the master bedroom, even though it's been over a year. Fifteen months to be exact. Donny says he can't smell it, but I think he just doesn't like the idea of breathing Joe Wycheski's cologne after sneaking into bed with his daughter.

I fell in love with Donny's skin first and moved in from there. The day he came to the front door he was brown with a flush underneath. He had gotten taller and full in the shoulders, his voice deeper in his chest. I hadn't seen him since school let out because I hadn't been able to go to the lanes—I wasn't ready for my father's picture on the wall with his hair slicked back and the smile he gave to people he didn't know.

It had been three months since my father had died, and Donny came to the door acting as if he'd just happened to notice the Wycheski lawn, even though it had been a wet spring and summer and his chinos were soaked to the knee. "On the side," he explained to me when he asked if he could help out with the mowing. He meant on the side from his jobs at the lanes and selling water softener and concentrated soap products to county people who have wells and brown teeth.

He came in for a glass of Vernon's and didn't look worried about breathing the air or sitting on our furniture like other people had, the few who visited after it came out why my father was sick. He borrowed his uncle Leo's tractor the first time, but after that he rolled his own push mower the three blocks and one street over to our house, and I watched him through the window or sat outside and pretended to read while he leaned on the mower, muscles moving under his skin. When he left the air smelled like wet soil and the grass tips gleamed like a million little lights.

Then fall came, and Donny asked me to go to the Cinema Six, and later we decided that if we still loved each other by graduation we would get married. Donny didn't mind my mother's tapes, and he said nothing when my mother started replacing my father's pastels with airbrushed pictures of Jesus walking in a crowd of children, preaching on the mount, crying on the cross.

I lock the master bathroom door, turn on the water, pull a single sheet out of the neatly slit envelope. Jake's letters are getting shorter. The first ones were three or four pages on both sides.

This one gets right to the point:

PAULA,

I DREAMED I SAW JESUS FLOATING OVER THE GARAGE AND I THINK IT MEANS WE SHOULD SKIP TOWN. MOVE ON LIKE JESUS, YOU KNOW? LIKE A ROLLING STONE. YOU'RE MY SPIRITUAL SOUNDING BOARD, HONEY, HOW YOU KEEP SAYING, BUT THERE'S MORE TO IT THAN THAT. NOBODY UNDERSTANDS ME BETTER THAN THAT. NOBODY UNDERSTANDS ME BETTER THAN YOU DO. ANYWAY, I NEED TO SEE YOU ALONE.

LILLY'S TAKING THE TWINS TO THE LAKE THIS WEEK. LET'S GO AWAY THIS WEEKEND AND FIGURE IT OUT. I'LL TELL HER I'M VISITNG MY MOTHER.

DON'T WORRY ABOUT TESS. THE MISSION WILL TAKE CARE OF EVERYTHING. I'LL MAKE SURE. I'LL CALL TOMORROW.

BLESSED BE THE LORD,
JAKE

I can see Jake scrawling in the toilet while his wife piles orange floatie wings and beach towels in the back of the minivan, the twins rolling around in the soft front lawn in matching outfits. Then I see us all together in Marietta, on top of the burial mound the Indians made, which is in the middle of town, me with a twin hanging on each hand, Jake with my mother on one side and his wife on the other. Trinities.

I slip the sheet back into the envelope. I stand in the shower, and what I want to know is, what exactly does Jake mean about the mission taking care of me?

I pull on my Eatery uniform over my still damp skin, pink skort sticking to my thighs, and shove shorts and a halter top into my pocket book. Through the vent a soothing male voice says, "Think of Christ as your friend who walks with you when you push your cart down the grocery-store aisles, when you get the paper, when you go to work." Music swells on the tape. Then I hear the squeak of Donny's brakes outside. "I'm going!" I call up the stairs.

No answer. I slam the door shut behind me. In the car, Donny leans across the seat to kiss me. He's redone his pony tail, name tag already attached to his turquoise-blue Star Lanes shirt.

"Do you have to do that?" I ask, pointing to it.

"I'll forget it if I don't." He puts his arm across the top of my seat as he backs down the driveway. I look at the veins running in blue ropes from his wrist to the inside of his elbow, where the skin is soft and white. It looks like a man's arm, like my father's arm, and it makes me ache.

Donny's smiling. "I sold three purification systems this week," he says.

I roll my eyes. "You know they don't do anything except add salt," I say. The company has this big color brochure on how it saves plumbing from mineral build up, but it really doesn't.

"You just can't stand it that people like this stuff."

"They like it but they don't need it. You tell them they need it."

"You're worse than Leo," Donny says, looking at me, trees blurring behind him. I try to stare back but I can't. I hate it when he gets mad at me. "Well, who got Leo to buy the new sound system and the laser and disco ball? Now you have to wait an hour for a lane on Friday."

"He just didn't want to go into debt."

"He's an old man, what does he know? He's still saving all his rubber bands off the paper in case there's another Depression. I guess we'll sell rubber bands then. Now, *that's* thinking."

"At least he's not a bullshitter!" I'm yelling now, my ears ringing.

"Oh, and I guess you got the corner on honesty. What about you and that scholarship deal, huh?" He slaps the wheel, shouts out a laugh. "Sitting there in your little uniform pretending to have a job."

"Asshole," I hiss.

"That's right," Donny says, voice low now, eyes steady on the road, jaw clenched. "I'm an asshole for trying to make my own way." Smoke slides out of his nostrils.

There's nothing I can say to this, except that I want college the way I wanted Donny last fall, when the nights got cooler and he didn't need to come over as often to mow, and he crawled in the window of the room my parents used to sleep in, and we undressed under the blankets, and our skin was so warm and slick against each other that we could have been under water.

Neither of us speaks until we get to the lanes. "I'm sorry," I finally say as he pulls into the gravel parking lot, even though I'm not sorry; I'm just tired, and I don't want to be angry. In front of us is the turquoise fan roof of the Star Lanes with the two round windows like eyes over the door. It's early yet, and there are only a few cars in front.

Donny opens the car door and stares ahead, one hand on the door handle and the other hanging down his thigh right at his crotch, the way guys do. Then he swings his legs out and slams the door behind him, walking away as if he had no one to wait for.

I lean across the seat and pop the trunk so I can get my ball. I can hear the hollow sound of the pins on the buttery wooden floor even before I open the glass doors. Then I pull the handle and the smell of leather and beer and sweat flows out on the cool air, although bowling doesn't make you sweat unless you're nervous. It's just the smell of men who come here every Friday and never air out their shoes. It's a good smell. And a good feeling to look across the lanes, the balls coursing down the boards, through the tunnel, out of the machine, and into the hands, circulating like air, like blood.

I change into my shorts and halter top in the bathroom and take a stool at the bar. Two guys I recognize from high school are drinking draft between rolls on the end lane, my father's favorite lane. Their girlfriends, or wives maybe, both pregnant, sit in the plastic booth, smoking, flicking ashes on the floor, permed hair teased up over pale foreheads, dark circles under their eyes. Staring at the balls going back and forth.

Leo comes over when he sees me, smiling. He's wearing his favorite Beers of the World shirt with all the labels in different languages and eating a bag of potato chips, even though he's supposed to be on a diet. He hands me a catalog, points to a picture of a smoothie machine.

"Tessie," he says, clapping my shoulder. "You think I should order this?"

"I don't know," I mumble.

"I think it's going to be the wave of the future. You can chop up candy bars in it." Leo smacks the magazine against his thigh. "Hey, sweets, what's the problem?"

I decide not to mention the fight with Donny. "My mother wants to move to Marietta."

Leo shakes his head, strokes his moustache. He looks across the lanes, to the lounge area, where the local branch of the Mafia used to entertain themselves after whacking members of the Polish contingency in Cleveland—this my father told me. Leo has never been one to ask for details. "Maybe she could go somewhere nice, like Atlantic City?" he says.

"I don't know what she's thinking, Leo," I tell him, and this is the truth.

"Could you check my math in a minute here?" Leo asks me.

"Sure thing."

"Maybe Florida?" Leo suggests as he heads to the back office.

My parents took me to Disney World on my eleventh birthday, the only time I've been out of Ohio. My dad chain smoked and bought me foam Mickey Mouse ears and called me Minnie all day, even after I lost the ears on the Witch Mountain roller coaster and cried, while my mother sat down every few feet, putting her head between her knees to keep from passing out in the heat. I used to keep a list of the best days of my life and this was at the top. I didn't want to leave, even though I was old enough to know that there were people inside the costumes and the park closed at night. "Just leave me here," I remember saying to my father. I can still see his face tilted down to mine, almost close enough to kiss me. But now I think his expression looked something like defeat.

The sun dips behind the buildings across the street and the white stones in the parking lot turn pale purple under the sky. More people are showing up, a couple of teams practicing for the next league event, some regulars who don't play for any team but come all the time. A shark or two scanning the talent. I find Donny at the control board in the DJ box. "Hey, can I come up?"

Donny pushes open the door without looking at me and turns back to the control panel. He's acting serious as an astronaut, when we both know he's only got one button and a joy stick.

"Donny," I say. "Don't be mad at me."

"For what?" he asks, looking distracted. He doesn't lose his temper often, and I can tell he's embarrassed. He pulls his chair closer to the board, surveys the stands below.

I want to say for leaving you. For putting you down even though I believe I'm right. For feeling like I see more than you can. Instead, I kneel behind him where no one can see me and press my face against the back of his neck until he turns enough to put an arm around me. We stay like that until Donny has to start the show.

It's after two when I'm helping Leo cash out in the office room—I'm doing change and he's doing bills. Donny's setting up for the next day. When we're done Leo pats a box of napkins beside him. I sit and wait until he's finished bundling the take. His face is deep red, hairlike veins fan from his nose. He smells like cigarettes and potato chips. He takes a deep breath, slaps his thick hands on his lap. "You know, Donny's like a son to me. His parents are ghosts," he says.

I keep my eyes on the coins. Leo's never talked this way to me before, like Donny's the child and we're the adults. In the whole time since I've known Donny, I've only seen his father once and his mother maybe a handful of times. They're both old; Donny has a brother and a sister that moved out ten years ago.

"You got a good head, Tess," Leo says, smoothing his gray mustache. "So I got an offer for you." I can feel his eyes on me, adding me up.

"Thank you," I say, feeling foolish.

"Year round work, good pay, full benefits."

"Doing what?"

"What you been doing. Helping me keep the numbers straight. You got a good head, Tess. You think about it." Leo waves me away and I get up to leave. I open my mouth to say something, but Leo lifts a hairy hand to stop me. "I'm glad Donny's got a girl like you. That's it."

When I wake up the next morning the house is hot and bright, and I'm alone. Upstairs, I peek in the doorway of my mother's room, and I can see the open closet, nearly empty except for her Sunday dresses and a neat line of shoes, and the TV in the corner on what used to be her bed stand, tapes stacked on the floor. I push open her door the rest of the way. Sitting in the center of her bed is a lavender duffel bag, open and waiting.

I check the coffee-table books for mail, but there's none. I shower and ride my bike to the high school, which is across the street from the cemetery, where my father is buried. In the hospital, when he knew before we were ready to admit it that he was going to die, he said he wanted to be cremated and scattered in Lake Erie; I remember the air in his voice, his hand on my arm, but my mother picked out the coffin and head stone as if he'd never asked for anything different. I wouldn't go there after the burial, even though I could see the marker from the school-bus window every day. Now Mr. Ontero is buried there, too, his tombstone bone white.

Mr. Todd's summer-school government class is just letting out. After my father died, Mr. Todd came by every few days with homework and lecture notes, so I kept up, and after a while I could have conversations again, and then I came back to school.

Mr. Todd sees me coming down the hallway and waves. He's younger than my parents, with a son in eighth-grade special ed and a fat wife with perfect creamy skin and red curly hair who always chaperones proms and wears the same cobalt-blue satin sheath dress with a black rose on one shoulder to every dance. Mr. Todd wears thick glasses and was probably a nerd in high school, but now he's a man, with sloping shoulders and beard shadow all of the time.

"Tess," he says, motioning me in. The last of the students file past us, all of them with bad cases of lecture face. He pulls a brown envelope from his desk and hands it to me. "Open it."

The letter starts with "Congratulations." I see the words "full tuition" and "special funds." There are several forms. Also a check made out to me for five hundred dollars. I bring the check, printed with an ocean scene, close to my face, studying Mr. Todd's leaning handwriting that I know so well from the margins of my papers, where he wrote, "Defend your pt. here" or "Don't leave me hanging." Ian and Leisel Todd, it says in the upper left hand corner, above the beach scene. I look at Mr. Todd and he smiles down at me as if I were his daughter, the way I believe my father would have smiled at me. I thank him, and he hugs me, and I hear his heart beating low in his chest, and what I feel is fear, and then relief.

"Let's go to lunch," he says.

He puts my bike in the back of his station wagon. The breeze bends the envelope forward in my hand, as if pushing me along. The rectangular brick building, the gravel teacher's parking lot, the line of pines edging the practice field all look familiar, but changed, flattened by my absence.

It's after three and the restaurants in town are closed until dinner. That's the kind of town this is. Mr. Todd brought in a writer from the *New York Times* to speak to our journalism class last year, a college buddy of his, and I remember him asking where a guy could get a late night cup of coffee around here, and we all stared back at him as if he'd asked where he could get laid.

We end up at Harry's. It's the first time I've been there since my father died. I wouldn't have gone in there if it weren't for the fact that I know I'm leaving now. I wanted to preserve his presence there, waiting for me. Mr. Todd orders, and I choose a booth in the corner, where my father and I almost never sat because you couldn't see the TV.

Mr. Todd buys a beer for himself and soda for me and two cold salami sandwiches. He sets my soda down and clinks the lip of his bottle against my can as he sits across from me.

"Thanks," I say. The backs of my thighs are sticking to the bench. I peel them up, settle them. We bite into our sandwiches. Mr. Todd drinks most of his beer in two long gulps.

"So. How do you feel?"

"Good. Nervous." The salami makes my eyes water and Mr. Todd notices, misreads it.

"Are you okay?" he asks.

I nod. He puts his hand heavily on mine and keeps it there. "How about your mom?"

I understand he's asking whether I've told my mother or not. He knows about our empty house and about Marietta, and about how my mom's job at the church day care doesn't pay the bills, and she was taking my tip money, which is how he came up with the scholarship in the first place. He knows enough about both of us to be my father. "She's having an affair with a married man," I answer, watching for his reaction.

He pulls his hand away, rubs his eyes. "Oh."

"She's going away with him this weekend."

"She told you?"

"No. But I know." I watch Mr. Todd pick at his beer-bottle label and I can tell he's trying to decide whether to ask about my sources. I debate whether I'll tell him about the letters and the duffel bag, about how Jake underlines for emphasis. But Mr. Todd doesn't ask. My legs are sticking to the seat again, and I squirm to adjust.

"The forms," he finally says, tapping the envelope. "Get those turned in right away."

I nod, and we finish eating in silence. Mr. Todd swallows the last of his beer. "Tess."

I look up from the crumbs on my napkin, waiting.

"Your dad and mom," he pauses, opening his hands as if to

catch the right words. "They're two extremes. You just shoot down the middle and you'll be fine."

Outside, Mr. Todd offers to take me back to the high school, but I tell him I'd rather ride. He pulls my bike out of his car. "Don't forget about me, now," he says, sounding something like my father and Donny combined.

When I get home I hear the shower running in the master bedroom, the metallic bird-call sound in the pipes. On the radio, the announcer's talking about a cold front; there'll be record lows. The AC is dry and cold on my skin; sweat rolls down my spine. I check the coffee-table books in the linen closet for mail, put the scholarship envelope in my backpack at the back of the my closet, and lie down on my parents' bed, listening to the water hit the floor of the bath tub.

When my mother opens the door, a cloud of steam behind her, she's startled to see me. She's got a pink towel around her middle and a white one around her head. Her face is shiny and flushed. "I was trying to figure out what you think is so great about this shower," she says.

"And?"

She shrugs. "Good water pressure. Better than upstairs. I'd forgotten." She unwinds the towel from her head and sits slowly on the edge of the bed, as if trying not to sink in too far. As the towel flops around her neck I see she's gotten a haircut and another dye job, so all the frizzy pinkish copper is gone, and the dark shiny hair drips in soft, water-slicked waves around her face. "What do you think?" she says, turning her head so I can see the back.

I sit up. "Are you going anywhere?"

My mother's eyes meet mine. She studies my face. "Where would I go?" she says. Her eyes narrow, searching. Maybe she thinks she isn't really hiding anything because her plans aren't firm, the bag is not yet packed. I don't answer, and she stands, looking down at me. "How about you?" she wants to know. "Where are you going?"

"I'm going to State," I tell her. My heart is pounding. My mother opens her mouth to speak, and then the phone rings. I am nearer to it but she reaches past me and picks up.

"Hello?" she says, turning her back to me, and I know she thinks it's Jake, hopes it's Jake. But then she turns and hands the phone to me.

"Donny," she says.

"Not the rolling stone?" I ask her, and I feel like I've jumped off a high dive, my stomach in my throat, my heart in my ears. I've shown my hand now; she knows what I know. My mother looks at me, sucks in air like she's been hit in the stomach, and I know she's putting it together, all the letters unfolded and refolded, all those words reread. I swing my legs off the other side of the bed and stand up, so the bed's between us. My mother isn't moving. I put the phone to my ear. Donny's saying, "Hello? Hello?"

"Yeah."

Donny can hear something's up from the tone of my voice. "Everything okay?"

"Great," I say with exaggerated cheer. "Are you picking me up?"

"I'll be there."

I listen for the click of the phone line, put the phone against my chest. My mother is watching me as if I'm someone entirely new to her. Her eyes are wide, almost amused. She turns and walks out of the room. Then I hear her running up the stairs.

I pull from the closet my backpack and my favorite jeans. I also pull all four of my father's bowling shirts, which I saved before my mother cleaned out his closet. I take some T-shirts, some underwear, a notebook I didn't use up all the way from the spring. And the pictures, one of my father and me at the Buckeye tournament, one at my graduation from junior high school, one of him holding me when I was a baby, his nose to my forehead. I slip them into the scholarship envelope so they won't bend. I change into my work clothes and I put the bag back in the closet, in the corner where it can't be seen even if the folding doors are open all the way.

I hear my mother going downstairs again and then to the kitchen. My hands feel shaky, weak, as I pick up my purse and bowling ball and carry them down the hall. My mother's chopping carrots for a salad. She seems perfectly composed, her hair gleaming under the fluorescent light. She doesn't look up when I come in. She slides the carrots into the bowl and puts the mushrooms under the faucet.

"I'm going to be late tonight," I announce.

My mother slices a tomato in two. "The house goes up for sale tomorrow," she says.

I wait for her to say more, to tell me the next step. I think of hot Marietta, where the Indians buried their dead, where white apartment buildings stand like grave markers. "Why now?" I ask. I hear Donny's car rolling up the drive.

"Saturdays are the best days to start," she says calmly, mis-understanding me on purpose. "There's going to be an open house on Sunday from two to five. I'll need your help."

"Would you like me to dust the couch?" I ask.

My mother glares at me. Donny honks the horn, and I bend to pick up my things. I look at my mother, her hand small on the knife, her hair dripping and quivering as she starts in on lettuce, pulling the good leaves away from the bad. I decide not to say goodbye.

In the car I tell Donny about the house and then the schol-arship. "Are you excited?" he asks me, even though he knows the answer.

"I'll have three roommates," I say. I reach for his hand. "Are you going to visit me?"

Donny rolls his eyes. "It's only two hours away."

This is true, but it feels farther. Donny drives with one hand and holds my hand until our palms are sticky and we can't feel the pressure on our skin anymore. I want him to say he'll go with me, find a job, save money for school. I want to cut his hair, buy him a suit, or even a nice button-down shirt. I want to tell him everyone will understand.

Donny pulls into the Star parking lot and cuts the engine, and we sit still as the car heats.

"Nothing's going to change," Donny says, and I believe him.

That night, Donny does a great show. You'd think it would be the same every night, but it's not. Sometimes the smoke rolls out evenly over the lanes like a piece of cloth, and the laser seems to become different things—a space ship, a man swimming, someone dancing. Tonight the music's from *Close Encounters of the Third Kind*, and people lean back on the booths, their faces open in the blue light. Donny makes the laser disappear and then reappear in a sweep that washes over us all. He makes it a knife, cutting light into the sky, then a layer of water that lifts above the lanes and spreads itself so thin it's nearly invisible.

I close my eyes and lean my head back and wonder what we look like from the air, from space. I see my father leaning out the window of his car to wave at me, gliding forward to roll. I just want to shoot down the middle, I tell him. The music gets louder until it pounds in my rib cage, and the laser breaks apart over the lanes, coming back together into a single glowing point and then goes dark. Everyone yells and claps.

Afterward, I help Leo serve up last beers and popcorns. In the control booth, Donny is shutting things down, the board lighting his face like a ghost. He sees me and waves, and I wave back, and then he turns off the desk light, and I can't see him anymore.

Then it's cash-out time. I hurry to the back room so I can get to Leo before Donny does. He's smoking a cigarette, which he quickly puts out, because it's against fire regulations to smoke around all the paper plates and napkins. "Tess!" he says, waving at the smoke as if he's just noticed it.

"Leo, I've got to ask you something."

"Ask."

"I got into school."

"I know."

This surprises me and then I realize Donny must have told him. "I want to know if I can come back. In case things don't work out."

"Oh, sure you can, Tess," Leo says. "But you won't." He pats my head with his paw hand, and I feel as if something has broken loose in my ribs, and then I'm crying into the brown polyester warmth of his shoulder until he helps me sit down.

"Breathe, sweetheart," he says. "Just breathe."

Then I feel Donny's hands on my arms, warm. "Let's roll some," he says.

I let him lead me into the dark lanes. We take my favorite one on the end, where I can concentrate. Donny puts change in the juke box and goes back up to his light board. He puts on the disco ball, white lights circling slow, like stars in a planetarium. I sit down, switch my shoes, pull my AMF out, and turn it in my hands. It's a little sparkling planet, all lakes and waves. I move to the head of the lane, shoes slick like a pillow of air. I pull in a deep breath, inhaling the place, which smells like wood and oil and beer and my father. I balance the ball and let its weight take my arm back, my body moving forward, my hand behind the ball, pushing it through the air. My thumb comes free and my hand turns into an almost handshake, fingers flicking the skin of the ball as it leaves them, all this in a split second, like air leaving the lungs, like a kiss.

I shut my eyes and bring my father's face close to mine, skin around his grey eyes crinkling. I'm leaving, I tell him, as the ball topples the pins. I know from the sound it's a strike.

By the time we get to my house it's very late. I make Donny stop several houses down the street from mine and turn off his lights. We sit there in the hollow car silence.

"What are we doing?" Donny asks.

"Shh." I get out quietly, shiver in the cool air. "Just wait for me here, okay?"

Donny nods and sits back. On my way down the street I glance at Mr. Ontero's dark house, the windows small and black. Every room is lit at my house, porch lights glowing over the For Sale sign leaning against the steps. My mother passes through the empty living room. She's wearing my pink sundress.

I wait until she walks upstairs and I let myself in the front door. There is the lavender duffel bag on the floor, full and zipped, the keys on the counter.

I head down the hallway and grab my backpack, checking for the envelope, my father's shirts, making sure it's all still there, ready. In the kitchen I hear my mother humming upstairs. I lift her keys slowly from the counter and pull the front door closed behind me.

I take the brick path around the side of the house to the edge of the woods and set down my backpack. The keys are cool in my hand. I hold them up to chin level, setting. My arm is trembling, tired but warm. I let it drop, fall back, my feet sliding with long, low strides, my arm swinging forward now, fingers relaxing on the upswing, then releasing the keys, which fly upward for quite a ways, because they are lighter than what I'm used to. They land somewhere in the dark trees with a muffled clink of metal. I listen to the quiet air for a moment and then walk back to the car, where Donny is waiting to take me to school.

MELISSA PRITCHARD
Writer

Interview

by Leslie A. Wootten

Disappearing Ingenue: The Misadventures of Eleanor Stoddard *is Melissa Pritchard's fifth book. It is her third collection of short stories, following* The Instinct for Bliss *(Zoland Books, 1995) and* Spirit Seizures *(University of Georgia Press, 1987). She has also authored two novels:* Phoenix *(Cane Hill Press, 1991) and* Selene of the Spirits *(Ontario Review Press, 1998). Her numerous honors for* Spirit Seizures *include the Flannery*

Melissa Pritchard

O'Connor Award, Carl Sandburg Award, James Phelan Award, *and an honorary citation from the PEN/Nelson Algren Award.* Instinct for Bliss *was a PEN West finalist and received the 1996 Janet Heidinger Kafka Prize for fiction by an American woman. In 1998, Pritchard was awarded a Howard Foundation*

Fellowship from Brown University to complete the Ingenue *collection of stories. Presently, she is an Associate Professor of English and Women's Studies at Arizona State University. She is also on the faculty at Spalding University in Louisville, Kentucky.*

How does Disappearing Ingenue *differ from your previous work?*

It's the most liberating of the books I've written, both personally and stylistically. With it, I celebrated autobiography, freely embellishing and exaggerating reality to achieve the dramatic—or comedic—effect I wanted. When I began writing years ago, the last thing I wanted was to write about myself. I wrote fiction to step away from my life, and that's why I often went as far afield as possible—fourteenth-century Poland, for example. The stories in *Spirit Seizures*—my first collection—were modeled after those written by authors I'd read and admired. I'd say, "Now, I'm going to attempt a Gogol, Tolstoy, Flaubert sort of story." Modeling my work on the stories of others was how I learned to write fiction. With my second collection, *Instinct for Bliss*, I left imitative writing behind for the most part. In fact, I let more of me seep in, particularly my spiritual beliefs. To do so was risky, because I didn't know if readers would welcome or condemn my foray into more personal and spiritual realms.

The stories in this collection deal with different stages of a woman's life; however, none hinge on the three most obvious female rites of passage: first menstrual period, childbirth, and menopause. Was it a conscious effort on your part to avoid writing about these particular transitions?

With this book, I was more focused on nonbiological rites of passage: the personal and private—often unspoken—rites that evolve from the pressures of society and family expectations. These subtle rites of passage often instill fear, shame, and silence in girls. When I was about six years old, for example, I had an Annie Oakley outfit I wore with great pride and joy. There's a photograph of me in chaps, vest, boots, cowboy hat, and holsters. I'm pointing my two cap guns at the camera with unabashed glee. Believe me, I'm not advocating violence or guns, but I clearly felt powerful as Annie Oakley. I loved the outfit, and wore it night and day, pointing those guns everywhere. The Annie Oakley phase got stamped out of me quickly, though. Another photograph features me at about the same age with an Easter basket. I'm wearing a frilly dress, Easter bonnet, patent-leather shoes, and ankle socks. The smile on my face isn't genuine like my Annie Oakley smile. Yet another photograph, same age, reveals me standing on a chair at the kitchen sink. I'm learning to wash dishes, and I'm wearing the right attire for the job: little apron tied around my waist, tiny rubber gloves. Again, the expression on my face doesn't come close to Annie Oakley delight. These are the rites of passages I was interested in—the ones that are planted in us without our even realizing what is going on. All I knew was that I loved the Annie Oakley outfit and I had to exchange it for frilly dresses and kitchen aprons. I couldn't put a finger on what was really happening at the time, but when those three photographs are side-by-side, the loss is clearly reflected in my face. I understand it now.

The first story in the book, "Port de Bras," involves the subtle rites of passage you're talking about.

Exactly. Eleanor's mother enrolls her in ballet so she can learn grace and poise. It's an appropriate activity for girls, but Eleanor struggles with ballet's rigid and unnatural poses. Meanwhile, she is voraciously reading books on the holocaust, trying to make sense of the horror. This kind of reading is not an approved activity, however. The librarian doesn't come right out and say it, but she disapproves mightily of Eleanor's reading choices. In a subtle way, Eleanor is made to feel that it is wrong for a proper twelve-year-old girl to fill her head with such atrocities. The unspoken message is clear: it's more important for a girl to have grace and good posture

186

than to contemplate world problems. In this, and each successive story, Eleanor grapples with expectations and roles that have been dropped on her.

"Port de Bras" is the only story told in first person. How did you decide what voice to use for this and other stories?

I generally decide how a story is going to be told before I begin writing. I run the story through different filters—first person, second person, third, listening to how each voice sounds, waiting until my body responds viscerally. When that happens, it's like a thrill of recognition. I say, "Oh, that's it," and it's almost always the voice I stay with. After listening and waiting, I heard "Port de Bras" in first person. Eleanor stepped on stage and began talking.

Discuss the visceral reaction you speak of.

I believe the physical body holds memory—and story. Actually, I'm convinced our bodies speak to us all the time, offering guidance in daily life. All we have to do is pay attention. In terms of writing, I rely on an internal ripple of intuition that manifests physically as a kind of charge in my solar plexus. With "Revelations of Child Love for the Soul of Dame Mi Mah," a story in *Instinct for Bliss*, I didn't initially wait long enough for my body to tell me what to do. Instead, I jumped into writing the story. After about five pages, I realized I wanted to be anywhere else—even grocery shopping, which I hate. Those pages got balled up and thrown away, and I did what I should have done to start with: I waited.

Describe the waiting process.

With "Revelations of Child Love," I waited in a state of tension for about two weeks, listening for the right voice. When I say voice, I mean point-of-view, but also narrative design—the story's architecture and organic form. The answer I needed came when I was at Mass. Good ideas have come to me when I've been in church. Instead of concentrating on the service, I was leafing through a hymnal. Suddenly, I knew the story would be in scriptural form. What evolved includes sixteen confessions—or revelations. It's about my mother. I wanted something that was sacred, but also funny. As with so many mothers and daughters, our relationship has been a mix of admiration and frustration, anger and joy, dislike and love. I wanted to strike a certain nerve on the page, but when I tried to write a conventional story, I couldn't get to the emotionally dangerous point I needed to get to. I had to wait for the right voice—the right form—that could carry the charge and danger this story needed.

Do you always know ahead of time what dangerous point you are aiming for?

No. Sometimes I have to write a draft or two to find it. I go by the same advice I give my students: if you aren't sure what the danger point is after finishing a draft, ask what secret you are keeping from yourself. My "secret" with "Revelations of Child Love" was I didn't want my mother to die—ever. She's still alive—eighty-four and practicing yoga—but I was full of anger and sorrow at the prospect of her eventual death. Once I understood what the story was about, I was able to anchor in and write fairly quickly.

Did you have a particular goal in mind when you set out to write this collection of stories?

I wanted to write a series of long short stories about a contemporary upper-middle-class white woman who eventually breaks free of familial and societal constraints. The arc I envisioned for the book included a gradual shift from enforced disempowerment that begins early in life to assertive self-confidence that develops over time.

You began writing these stories shortly after finishing your Victorian novel, Selene of the Spirits. *How did you emotionally shift from the nineteenth century to the twentieth century of* Disappearing Ingenue?

I leaped joyfully into "Funktionslust," reveling in the opportunity to write any way I wanted. The story is me doing verbal cartwheels after mincing along in the stiff corset of

Victorian language. It's also my personal declaration of independence as a writer and a woman.

Although you wrote the story first, it's the book's finale.

Yes. "Port de Bras" begins the book and "Funktionslust" ends it. The two stories make contrasting bookends that emphasize how Eleanor changes through the decades of her life. In "Funktionslust," Eleanor finally embraces her own authentic voice and spirit. As she approaches her fifth decade, she becomes an incarnation of the empowered Annie Oakley, literally disappearing and lofting into myth. She almost has to become a mythical figure.

"Larger than life" mythical, wouldn't you say?

Yes. Eleanor sets off on an adventurous journey—a new life of her own choosing. In writing this particular story, my own wild womanhood established sure footing. I, too, set off on an adventurous journey—the journey of writing in a way that was new and liberating for me.

There's a double edge to the word "mythical," isn't there?

That's right. Simply put, there's no suitable place for Eleanor in contemporary society. After forty or fifty years, the ingenue role wears mighty thin. It actually doesn't even apply to many women of her generation—myself included. After years of raising families largely on our own, we're independent and assertive. Finally, we're ready to throw off the ingenue shackles and become "wild women." But, what do we do? Where do we go? There are seldom any available men our age to be wild with. Often, we end up alone or with younger men who aren't threatened by female strength because they have been raised by divorced single mothers who had to be strong. After contemplating the various men available to her, Eleanor embarks on her journey without one.

The stories are connected—that is, Eleanor is the main character in each. They are, however, stylistically quite different from each other.

With each story I set different goals for myself. With "Funktionslust," I went barking mad with language. In "Salve

Regina," the risk was to write a conventional, deliberately slow-paced story that was boring without being boring. At first, I worried that people would be bored reading the story because I was faintly bored writing it. After my metabolism slowed, and I settled into the molasses of writing the piece, I could see it was richer than I originally thought. Audiences have responded well when I've read it, probably due—in part—to its leisurely, organic rhythm.

It's certainly rich and sensual. Did you set out to write a story that specifically pairs religion and sensuality?

Absolutely. "Salve Regina" is a coming-of-age story that includes first betrayals and actual seductions. Eleanor and her friend Lacey are students at a Catholic girls school. Lacey is seduced by an older boy and eagerly loses her virginity; in contrast, Eleanor aspires to become a chaste saint by denying her body. I wanted to evoke a combination of the spirit yearning for God versus the body yearning for biological union. Catholicism as a backdrop provided the right setting to accomplish these goals, mainly because Catholicism is itself a form of physical seduction—a feast for the senses—that strives to reach the spirit through the body.

There's a great deal of humor in these stories. Were you consciously weaving humor in or was it a serendipitous by-product?

With every book I've tried to challenge myself. In this collection, I let the humorous and comedic side of me loose. I wasn't sure readers would share my sense of humor. I think "Funktionslust" is hilarious, but I was terrified at my first reading of it because I didn't know how the audience would react. In fact, there was an elderly couple present, and my prim convent-self stepped forward and apologized for anything in the story that might offend. Luckily, the elderly couple laughed harder than anyone and came forward afterwards to tell me they weren't offended at all. Their positive reaction encouraged me to continue including humor in my stories.

I laughed throughout "The Case of the Disappearing Ingenue."

With that story, humor was the best way for me to approach an actual murder that had intrigued me for years. The man who was eventually convicted of killing candy heiress Helen Brach managed the horse stable where my daughter took lessons. At the time, he hadn't been arrested, but there was speculation that he was the murderer. I was fascinated with the rumors. At one point after he'd been tried and convicted, I toyed with the idea of writing a grim, gothic story about the case, but I never could bring myself to do it. At some point, I started thinking maybe I could get at him through humor—Nancy Drew humor—and I played a "what-if" game. What if a bored housewife decides to don a disguise and go sleuthing to determine if the stable manager murdered the heiress? What if the housewife gets in over her head, and the whole thing gets too close for comfort? Humor was definitely the way for me to go here.

The grim, gothic story in this collection is "The Widow's Poet."

Yes, and I have to say it's something of an anomaly. Humor isn't key in this story as it is in so many of the others.

In "The Widow's Poet," Eleanor's brooding young lover, Christian, tells her he is reading "the de Sade book." Was de Sade's iconoclastic philosophy on your mind as you wrote this psychologically rich story?

To a certain degree, yes. I'd just finished reading Francine Prose's *At Home with the Marquis de Sade.* I had also been reading a great deal of gothic fiction for a writing class I was teaching, and I thought, hmm, I want to see if I can write a story that will scare me to death. That was the main challenge of the story, but I also wanted to explore issues of women's sexuality that aren't generally considered, such as the Jungian notion that we subconsciously attract people into our lives who represent our shadow. Through Christian, Eleanor is transported to terrifying psychological depths.

It's scary to read.

The story was scary to write, especially towards the end

when I had no idea what was going to happen. I actually had to force myself to continue because I was so afraid of what I would discover as I moved forward. Kind of like Bluebeard—don't open that door because you'll see corpses hanging in the closet. I'd open a door and there would be a smaller, darker door, then another and another. I really had to summon all my courage to make it to the end.

How did you feel after the story was over?

I felt unhinged, almost crazy for having written it. Self-censorship immediately started swirling in my head. I worried what people would think of me when they read it and whether anyone would publish it. Eventually, I was able to face down my fears, and tell myself that I can write anything I want if I'm willing to take responsibility for it. The decision was liberating. As it turned out, *Boulevard* published the story, and it was nominated for a Pushcart Prize. It was probably the hardest story I've ever written, but with it—as with "Funktionslust"—I was able to break free of inhibiting rules I'd subconsciously set up for myself.

Most of the stories occur in linear time except for "Her Last Man" which is in what I'll call "felt time." Could you talk a bit about the construction and composition of that story?

First of all, the story is about my father. It's my love story for him, like "Revelations of Child Love" is a love story for my mother. I knew I couldn't—and didn't want to—write a traditional father/daughter piece. A great deal of raw emotion was involved, and I needed a different way in. The episodic format presented itself when I realized that memories of my father are stored in my mind—and body—as individual scenes in bundled nodes of memory. Once I discovered the right form—jazz-like episodic vignettes—the writing flowed quickly.

Didn't the story go on to have a life of its own?

Yes. A friend who read it remarked that it just had to be performed. She said she could visualize it, see the costumes, performers, everything. Although theater was not at all on my mind when I wrote the story, I was intrigued by the idea. What resulted was an amazing ensemble production that included four women poets and myself performing father-daughter reflections we'd written. It was really quite moving. And fun.

Eleanor seems lonely much of the time even though she has many friends. Could you discuss the dichotomy between her social and private being?

I don't think Eleanor is ever truly lonely, but she is often alone, and she does meditate—even as a young girl—on her life. Buddhism talks about that: we are all alone, yet we are also all connected. A fiction writer can make room—and time—for characters to reflect on life by slowing down their internal clocks. That's a luxury we don't really have in our day-to-day lives.

Eleanor is confronted with loss in every story, and although the losses are traumatic, they do not ultimately debilitate her. She discovers unexpected and unconventional ways to cope at every stage of her life. Could you comment on what I see as Eleanor's irrepressible resilience?

I wanted her to be resilient. She needs to be. It's a fact of life that hearts are broken again and again in different ways. We lose loved ones; our dreams our dashed. The key to growing as a human is to understand that, yes, hearts break, but they break open. With each breakage, we become more fully human. On some level every story is a story of love, as well as one of innocence. Eleanor's heart breaks in some way in each story, but the experiences help her grow and understand as well as appreciate life more fully. There's a French saying that—roughly translated—says: "To understand is to forgive. To forgive is to heal." If Eleanor can understand, she can forgive. If she can forgive, she can heal. It's true for her—and all of us.

What do you mean by the word "innocence"?

As we move through life, we're always innocent of what is

next. For example, on my dad's eightieth birthday, I asked him how it felt to be an octogenarian. He laughed and said, "How would I know? I've never been eighty before." Now that he's eighty-four, he might be able to answer the question, but not then. Another example of our innocence is connected to the death of loved ones. There is no training for this. Many of my friends' mothers have died lately. Such loss is a rite of passage that we can't know—or understand—until we experience it ourselves.

Although your characters often live outwardly conventional lives, it seems that conventional solutions do not ultimately satisfy them. Could you discuss the accuracy of this observation?

My characters are on missions to get at the truth, whatever the truth is. Their ultimate challenge is to understand life. When they're on a mission of this sort, they can't stay within convention very long. They may eventually return to convention, but only after they've explored beyond it. To return home, they must first leave it. To truly learn, they must make mistakes. My characters are on journeys, and their travels take them to actual foreign countries or foreign realms of the mind. They are strangers visiting places they've never been. I want them to take risks, to be confronted by temptation, to touch the forbidden, to break taboos. In the *Ingenue* collection, Eleanor journeys farther with each story into new territory that vitally challenges and tests her in some way.

Your women characters often have lives that include traditional female activities involving home, marriage, and children. These same women are typically strong, appealing, and frequently funny. When you set out to write a story, are you consciously juggling feminine and feminist?

Although I don't consciously think in terms of feminine versus feminist when I'm writing, I can see that I juggle the two in my life as well as my fiction. I feel like I've been moving through life with a high heel on one foot and a cowboy boot on the other. It's incredibly awkward, but humor-

194

ous at the same time. This combination of awkwardness and humor is key in the *Ingenue* collection. I think other women, particularly of my generation, have felt something similar to what I've felt. Various subtle permutations of the mismatched footwear play out in so many of our relationships and activities. For example, I'll sometimes write all morning and spend the afternoon doing domestic chores such as washing dishes or laundry. I often welcome the humble activity of such chores after hours of exhausting mental work. Part of the challenge in all this is knowing what to keep and what to let go of. I'm well versed in the domestic arts, but even though I know how to fold fingertip towels, I don't own any and wouldn't fold one if I did. I know how to iron hankies and shirts, but I seldom iron anything anymore. Writing, especially with humor, helps me keep it all in perspective.

Is this collection for men as well as women?

First of all, it's for me—to resolve questions about my own life: what I've been taught, what I've learned. It's also for women who have been moving through life wearing mismatched shoes, women who were raised to emulate the 1950s image of Betty Crocker, but who were rocked by the feminist movement that took hold in the 1970s. It's for the daughters of these women, as well. The collection isn't just for women, though. It's certainly for those men who want to better understand women. The stories are not feminist diatribes; hopefully, they revolve around human relationships and life experiences that men as well as women can relate to.

In "Hi Fidelity," Eleanor's daughters, Suave and Prell, as they call themselves, are opinionated, strong, and independent. They aren't going to struggle with the same issues Eleanor has been confronted with, are they?

No, and that's one of the points I wanted to make with the story. Suave and Prell haven't been placed under the same ingenue bell jar as their mother. Consequently, they are much truer to their individual natures, more free-spirited and uninhibited than Eleanor was at their age. I raised my own daughters, Noelle and Caitlin, to have a similar kind of self-assurance. It has made for some humorous situations in our household, because I still have some of the old Eleanor Stoddard stuff going on. For example, every now and then, I try to have a formal dinner when both daughters are at home. Real 1950s style with candles, china, cordial conversation. The minute we sit down, the entire plan disintegrates because my daughters immediately begin joking around and telling funny stories. This happens with or without guests. For a minute or two, I'm perturbed and try to gain control of the situation, but then I remind myself that I raised my daughters to be high-spirited. At that point, I settle down and join the fun.

Are names a clue to your characters?

Yes. Eleanor's variety of names reflects the many transformations and incarnations she goes through in her various decades of life. As a girl, nicknames are often dropped on her, and she rolls right along with them. Jaz, for example, is what her father calls her, and she never knows why. Moo, Mooser, Nors, and Noser are nicknames friends give her. The various married names—Eleanor Luther, Nora Bettinger—are representative of how women—particularly of my generation—were trained to trade-in their own last names for their husband's. If you divorced and remarried, you simply traded names again, kind of like trading baseball cards. Pearl Marvel is a nom de plume from Eleanor's brief stint as a romance writer. The name "Nora" materializes as she gains maturity and a greater sense of self.

In "Virgin Blue," Eleanor dresses in her "newest thrift-store finds, a parochial school blouse and vintage circle skirt, handpainted labial pink with sudsy palm trees." This is just one example of many intricately detailed outfits. Could you discuss the significance of clothing in this story collection?

When I was involved with theater years ago, I learned that clothing is a visual language all its own—a language that reveals essential information about characters and how they perceive themselves. Eleanor changes her clothing according to how she feels about herself as she moves through life. Her outfits are clues to her ever-evolving self-image.

It's clear from the book's wild garden of vocabulary that you are passionate about words. I can open the book anywhere and pick out rich phrases such as "rumps like underripe apricots bouncing against the saddles" and "her single braid like a gold belt snapping the dirt." Do such images come easily or do you have to audition words until they fit together in uniquely vivid ways?

I'm convinced language is the repository of the senses. I've always loved language, especially metaphor and imagery. Before I wrote fiction, I wrote poetry. If I could paint, I'd be a visual artist. To answer your question, though, I work the language hard to get the descriptive phrases I want. Often, images materialize during the revision process when I tend to use associative language and pair images in unexpected ways. The underripe-apricot image is a good example of how my mind works during this process. When my older daughter took riding lessons years ago, I spent hours watching her and other seven- and eight-year-old girls bounce up and down in tight beige jodhpurs. Their tiny behinds looked exactly like apricots to me. I knew apricots well because as a child, I had to pick hundreds of them off our backyard tree. The two dissimilar images fit together to accomplish what I wanted. I don't know how brain chemistry works—whether my ability to combine unlikely images is a gift or something I trained myself to do. I am clumsy, but observant.

What are you writing now?

I'm finishing a contemporary novel that explores the myth of romance versus the truth of love. For me, it's another highwire act without a net because the novel is arranged in serious, grim, and humorous sections that aren't necessarily cohesive.

Do you read when you are writing?

Definitely. When I'm working on a project as I am now, my reading choices usually inform my writing in some way. For example, I just finished a new translation of Tolstoy's *Anna Karenina*. Tolstoy is a master at opening up moments and taking time to leisurely follow a character's thoughts and actions. His contemplative style encouraged me to slow down and open up moments in my own novel. *The Penguin Book of Irish Fiction* is the next book I'll read.

Is there anything I didn't ask that you'd like to say?

Only that I truly believe stories repose deep within our flesh, and it's crucial for us to find ways to release them. If we don't let our stories speak, they can create physical and emotional disturbances within us. My release is a balance of meditation, dance, reading, and writing. This combination of mind, body, and spirit keeps me healthy and fuels my desire to take risks in my writing life.

Leslie A. Wootten lives and writes on a farm in Casa Grande, Arizona. Her work has been published, or is forthcoming, in *Tin House, Missouri Review, Bloomsbury Review*, and elsewhere.

The

Last

Pages

Elisabeth Giffey Burmeister and friend.

CHIEH CHIENG

*B*ack in ninety-eight, my parents wanted to have another big family trip. I had just graduated from college and was excited about going on a vacation, but not with my parents and older brother.

My mother attempted to cheer me up on the flight to Malaysia. She told me that after I was born, my grandparents in Sibu had asked if they could have me. They'd said to my mother, "If you leave him here with us, you can go back to work. You wouldn't have to stay home to take care of him."

My parents ultimately decided not to give me away, despite my grandparents' promise that, as a child of the eldest son, all of Sibu would be mine and I'd be treated first among my many cousins.

After she finished the story, my mother said, "Well, aren't you glad we decided to keep you?"

When I landed in Sibu, I saw the beautiful roads, trees, and rivers, and I couldn't keep from thinking, "This all could have been mine."

LISA GRALEY

I could not wish anyone a happier childhood than one spent in the company of goats. My father bought goats for my brother and me when we were children. Sometimes we herded them onto my grandparents' second-story, front porch. They were affectionate playmates who, incidentally, taught us to jump from that height. Though this was scary, my mother must have sensed its inevitability and let it happen. Tasting freedom as kids, the goats never stayed in the fence as adults, and the neighbors, Mortana or Gladys, sometimes phoned to say they were out.

As a newspaper reporter, I kept track of the folks who had goats, and on days when the world was too much with me, I stopped to visit—at Paul Thomas's, or Tina Black's father's farm. Being with the goats put things right again. Even today, when I drive by a friendly seeming herd of goats, I take pictures. My friend Esther and I once used a whole roll of film for a goat tied on someone's porch.

Point is, some great storytellers—Esther, my grandparents, my great-aunts, and my cousin Elaine among them—have goat stories in them. It seems a good starting place.

Our first goat, Mama, died while giving birth to four white goats. We fed the kids simultaneously with a wooden crate my father rigged to hold four RC Cola bottles with rubber nipples. Pictured are Tummy, Billy the Kid, Sugar, and Queen.

*I*n a box of forgotten photos, I found my silhouettes, rendered years apart. What strikes me is the similarity of my face over time, how certain things about my profile have not changed. In these silhouettes, I see the immutable features handed down to me. There are Dad's eyebrows, Mom's smile, Charlie's hips and flat thumbs, Grandmother's eye color—or is it Dad's? I comprehend my writing in the same way. It is my individual voice, a communicator to the world—much like my face.

But writing is also collaboration, a layering of teachers' lessons throughout my life. First, there was my mother, who wrapped her mouth around interesting words and asked tour guides probing questions. Then, there was my Grandmother Beth, the artist, who pointed out a thousand different shades of green in the treetops. And, to this day, I can read a paragraph and hear a chorus of many wise writing teachers and fellow students. So, in the end, my stories are like my silhouettes. They are a part of me, they go deep, yet they are also a projection of all that I am and all that I've been given.

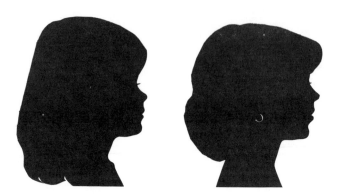

QUINN DALTON

I started "Midnight Bowling" to poke fun at people who subscribe to the showier brands of religious expression. Living in the South most of my life, I've come across it a lot—the coworker's restaurant birthday lunch where the boss asked everyone to hold hands and pray, the scripture-quoting storekeeper, teetotalers' weddings. I wanted to laugh it off with this story (though I set it in the North). But then it became something more for me and for these characters: a yearning for comfort.

Although I grew up, married, and baptized my daughter in the Episcopal Church, I can't honestly say I'm a believer. I'm just not one to turn away a prayer sent in my direction. My religious friends now know better than to ask if I pray, but recently I realized that in fact I do. Raising my daughter is a daily act of faith and hope.

N. S. KÖENINGS

*T*hese are the tools I want to write with: binoculars, a microscope, a stopwatch, a wall clock and a calendar, a scalpel and a comb, hair oil, and a tiny, golden pair of scissors which must be very hard to hold. This story is for my parents, who have been wonderful.

At Walden Pond, 1999.

"M.G.'s Parlor" by N.S. Köenings

LAURENCE DE LOOZE

*I*n 1982 I had a "working scholarship" to the Breadloaf Writers' Conference. I had never been to a writers' conference, nor even taken a class in fiction writing. Two things happened there.

The first is that John Gardner gave a workshop in which we had ten minutes to write something, as he put it, "overtly political." I raced back to my room and scribbled two pages about an arrest in a fruit market in Ceaucescu's Romania. I had spent the summer of 1980 there, and I had seen some things. When I ran back, it turned out I had taken fifteen minutes, and the workshop was over. But I found Gardner and read him what I had written. He asked to buy it for his journal, *MSS*.

Four days later, John died in a motorcycle accident. I couldn't bring myself to cash in on his offer, so for four years I did nothing. Finally I wrote his widow. All she said when she read the piece was, "We still want it." I learned from Gardner (also Carolyn Forché) that political writing can be beautiful.

The second thing is that at Breadloaf I was assigned as a roommate the wonderful Indian-American poet, Agha Shahid Ali. He knew hundreds of poems by heart and would recite them in the dark after lights out. Shahid died of a congenital brain tumor in December 2001.

This story is a companion to an earlier *Glimmer Train* story about Argentina. Like the first one, this lay dormant on my desk for five years because I didn't think it was any good. Many of the events in "Berlin Story" happened to people I either know or know of. And the rest of the events may well have happened to people unknown to me.

I dedicate this story to my Argentine wife, Rosa, who was there in Guillermo's apartment the day the paramilitaries showed up. And to Shahid, who wasn't.

ZOË GRIFFITH-JONES

*F*or several years, many years ago, I worked for a small but vibrant weekly newspaper in a small but diverse hamlet in Northern California. The pay was subsistence level, the hours illegal, and job descriptions could not be summed up briefly. My job was photographer, reporter, paste-up person, ad designer, and copy editor. I loved it immensely, and was heartbroken when increasingly frequent bounced paychecks required that I seek profitable employment.

But while it lasted, and despite its meager budget, the paper was a creative hothouse and, best of all, *fun*. We weren't above placing phony ads for "speed listening" seminars, or printing grossly unflattering photos of local dignitaries. From time to time I penned a tongue-in-cheek society column under the *nom de plume* "Miranda Trifly-Underbilt," and eventually Miranda graced the community with public appearances at select uptown soirées.

Here is Miranda in one of her stunning ensembles, escorted by (the alter-ego of) her friend Connie.

I have two thoughts about Miranda: One, I can't believe I did that, and two, I'm really glad I did.

$\mathcal{A}$t the time I was writing "Lists," I was also working towards a graduate degree in Asian American Studies at UCLA, doing research on the new wave of Japanese immigrants who have come to America in the past few decades (my mother being one of them). It seems to me that when you move to another country there are always pressures to adapt to your new environment, but that there are also pressures to remain as much the same as possible, to preserve everything you brought with you: your language, history, and social customs—the sense of who you were in your homeland. These pressures are different for each person depending on circumstances of gender, economics, culture, and age, and it is the idea of negotiating these complex forces that serves as the basis for my story. Ultimately, though, wherever they end up living, people do what they need to do, what they feel is truest to themselves and the life they are meant to lead.

Dabby, 1951.

Coming soon:

Rhea passes one of the shoes to Phil, who raises it to his nose and sniffs. The gesture endears him to me absolutely. In this visual world, this modern landscape of chrome and linen, leather and pigment, it is smell that most retains vestiges of the living.

from "Madrigals for a Bauhaus Baby" by Karen Kovacik

With an irresistible lightness, he let himself rise with the heat and the flames towards the sky. He raised his arms from his sides and relinquished himself to heat and sky, following the channel of fire higher and higher toward a purple yonder.

from "Morning Prayers" by Christopher Bundy

Caleb turned to run toward the cottage, but our three moms were already descending the trail. Aunt Dee Dee led them as always. Her flip-flops slapped happily, but her furious eyes were locked on Uncle Lucien.

from "Sand Thieves" by Adam Schuitema